STRIVERS

and other stories

STRIVERS

and other stories

ROBERT J. WILLIAMS

Washington Writers' Publishing House
Washington, DC

THIS IS A WORK OF FICTION

Copyright © 2016 by Robert J. Williams
All rights reserved

COVER DESIGN: Denise Nielsen

COVER ART: *Pullman Porter,*
Copyright © 2015 by Dana Ellyn
(www.danaellyn.com)
Reproduced by permission.

AUTHOR PHOTO: Zori Studios

BOOK DESIGN and TYPESETTING: Barbara Shaw

ISBN 978-1-941551-11-0

LIBRARY OF CONGRESS CATALOGUING-IN-PUBLICATION DATA
Names: Williams, Robert J., 1969- author.
Title: Strivers and other stories / Robert J. Williams.
Description: Washington, DC : Washington Writers' Publishing
    House, 2016.
Identifiers: LCCN 2016031850 | ISBN 9781941551110 (pbk. :
    alk. paper)
Classification: LCC PS3623.I5623 A6 2016 | DDC 813/.6—dc23
LC record available at: https://lccn.loc.gov/2016031850

Printed in the United States of America

WASHINGTON WRITERS' PUBLISHING HOUSE
P. O. Box 15271
Washington, DC 20003

For my parents

CONTENTS

Some Get Back	9
Assisted Living	22
The Benefactress	33
Love You. Always	46
Collier Road	57
The Photograph	71
Cotton Compress	84
Glass House	97
Just Desserts	108
Tea Time	120
Dates for Kreeger	133
Crystal Lake	147
Strivers	159
The Interview	177
Lester is Late	205
Acknowledgements	217

Some Get Back

(1938)

The smell of Kimball's Bakery was the best part about working there. Cozy blankets of warm dew draped its red brick walls, emitting the permanent aroma of yeast, butter, and sweet mystery spices. The worst part about working there: everything else. Mr. Kimball saw to that. A scrawny snatch of a man with oily black hair and a slivery mustache, he cared little for the breads and other baked goods he'd learned how to create years before in the kitchen of the old Kimball home that abutted the bakery's modern industrial building. Saved from demolition, the family's cottage stood as an empty and unused vestige of humble beginnings, a visual testament from whence the hardworking and stoic Kimballs came.

Nostalgia and pride failed to inject any cheer towards the business Mr. Kimball had been destined for since teething on day-old sourdough. Humorless workdays began with a mid-morning stroll, a ritual where the emperor surveyed his kingdom with folded arms and delivered stern, wordless lectures by way of steely glares. At sweaty workers who were supposed to be tending to the ovens instead of wasting time with chatter. At beggars and hobos, holding out eager hands

9

awaiting free samples. At reptilian creditors making surprise visits to surreptitiously investigate rumors of a lull in business. And especially at the shifty delivery boys—all colored—who came in too early for their own good, filling the rear dock with their cheap cigarette smoke, childish contests of strength and lies about what they'd seen and what they were going to do in life. Solomon Gray was one of them, often referred to collectively as The Boys, or individually by their first name appended with their delivery territory. Charlie *Broad Street*, Billy Lee *Gwinnett Street*, Jimmy *Milledgeville Road*. In his nasty squawk, Kimball would cry out such concocted brands during a morning roll call, his eyes never rising from an ever-present clipboard cutting across his frail chest cavity.

Solomon inherited The Hill route a month after his own father keeled over and died after rushing to unload a crate of bread at a store on Central Avenue. This forced Solomon to pass daily the very stoop where his daddy took a final breath. During deliveries, the foggy-brained old white storekeeper often revisited the excitement and sorrow of the day.

"Bless his heart," the old man would say, shaky brittle fingers fiddling between the loose openings of his button shirts, "your papa grabbed his chest and just plopped right atop sixteen loaves of sandwich bread right there." He'd nod towards the steps and outline a hefty body shape with his forefinger. "Mashed 'em plum flat with all that weight he toted around. Took four strapping men to lift him up, and when they did, you could see the impression he made on all that good bread. But he went to Glory doing what he loved the most."

Loving delivering baked goods? For a tyrant? That was a crock, and Solomon knew that somehow the old man knew that too, addled mind and all. During such exchanges, Solomon had taken to squeezing his hands to relieve kinks formed by gripping crates all day long and repress urges to say or do something out of line in the presence of white customers.

Respite was to be found at the last stop of the day, Ledbetter's Grocery, tucked away on a dusty side street that snaked down the backside of The Hill, a residential slope dotted with homes and shacks owned and rented by colored folks of all classes. The confines of Ledbetter's kept those who lived nearby—or worked all day in the cotton mills or for rich white people on the front side of The Hill—close-knit, protected, and shielded from the Mr. Kimballs and white storekeepers of the world. For a nickel, Solomon would buy a discounted RC, a handful of gingersnaps, and a moment of Ledbetter's time. Then later in the evening, after his workday ended, Solomon would return again, a free man for another few hours; free to spend his nickels on more flat soda pop and stale cookies, listen to boxing matches on the radio, and hear the same stories of misery and happiness retold over and over again. Ledbetter himself arbitrated the discussions, vetoing topics too upsetting to his missus or too blue for his young, spoiled-rotten children, who had the run of the place and whose hands were allowed to roam the candy jars and cookie racks, or even change the tuner on the radio without asking anybody grown.

On a breezy autumn Friday evening, with the colored mill workers nearby divvying up corn liquor in preparation for a weekend of aimless carousing, the subject of business, in particular the state of Kimball's, found its way into the succession of the day's topics.

Ledbetter peered over *The Chronicle's* business page, filled up with tables of stock exchange quotes, some circled in blue ink to track the returns on imaginary investments. "How's things looking over there at Kimball's?" Ledbetter asked.

"What I know, boss," Solomon said, dropping his tongue into lazy slow talk. "I just tote the bread, avoid Kimball like he is the Devil himself, and take home a few bills to my kinfolk each week. I don't know nothing about the man's pecuniary affairs."

"You know how much work you delivery boys got, which is indicative of how much business Kimball has."

"Well, the work ain't change. Still more of it than there is men."

"I just hear stories, is all. Saying things ain't how they used to be. Young Kimball is ruining the place, mishandling the books, killing off his old steady flow of good customers. Lots of people are going with the new place down there on Jones Street."

Solomon knew Ledbetter's sources. He sucked ginger-snap crumbs from his teeth and shot a dismissive look. "You listening to the secondhand information them caddie boys scrounge up off from the golf course? Again? They don't understand half of what they think they be hearing."

"I'm just asking. Might be time for me to change up. We've been giving Kimball's good steady business for twenty years. And not once, not one single time since the boy done took over have I gotten so much as a courtesy visit. 'How's my product? What's selling? What the colored folks on the back of The Hill wanting these days?' Not once. Just deliveries and invoices is all I get."

"And you got such pleasant correspondence before? From the old-folk Kimballs?"

"Not exactly. But I suspect, with times changing the way they are ..."

Solomon reached for a section of the newspaper, its broadsheets strewn about Ledbetter's countertop. He pointed at the date on the masthead. "1938? Might as well be 1838 to Kimball and the white folks in this town. One day though, you'll see; things is going to change."

That prophecy had been uttered often in Ledbetter's store, with little evidence hinting at its potential accuracy.

"Turn on the fights, why don't you," said Solomon. "Let my mind drift to someplace where a colored man will come out on top tonight, somewhere in this great big old world."

Ledbetter rolled the heavy radio dial until the tuner honed in on a raspy announcer's voice carrying on about a shower of rights and lefts and jabs and hooks his unbelieving eyes were witnessing.

"There you go." Solomon leaned back and rested his head peacefully in his interlocking hands.

The following Monday found Kimball in a terrible mood, his ire targeting a fallen flour sack that lay busted open and, from it, a ten-yard trail of whiteness lining the bakery floor. Kimball could see no accident, just the loss of profits from a couple of crates of bread. Some of the boys figured it was a deliberate sabotage job. Curses dripped from Kimball's little mouth.

"You boys need to come in here and clean up!" he shouted out to the dock. "Right this minute!" Anger elevated the pitch of Kimball's voice, making him sound more shrill and effeminate than usual. The boys filed in and snapped into an orderly row, shoulder to shoulder.

"Boss, that ain't exactly our job," Horace *Pinched Gut* said. His fat tongue choked over his words, but Kimball heard them clearly. He fired Horace right there on the spot. Horace's eyes sank, and a single tear slowly cascaded down the side of his billowing cheek, giving way to sniffles and futile pathetic apologies. Solomon and the boys shook their heads in unison and shuffled backwards, away from Horace, leaving him standing at the apex of a prayerful semi-circle of shame. Kimball just stood there, arms flapping like a jaybird's wings, telling a man nearly double his size that the best steady job he'd known was history and the next boss he had would hardly be so kind.

Horace was weak-minded, but not fragile. He had no wife, no children, and more tragic and unpredictable roadblocks in the path of his life than losing a two-cent piece of a job. But something in Kimball, something beyond his whiteness, had the capacity to break a man down. Solomon never saw a grown colored man cry until that day.

"Get on. Sobbing ain't going to do you no good now," Kimball said. He showed Horace the door, and handed brooms to the boys, who swept the morning away in silence.

"Man is evil," Solomon said to Ledbetter after recounting the story later that evening. "Somebody ought to teach him a lesson. Show him how it feels to be on the other end of that mean stick."

Ledbetter smiled. "You new Negroes. Got puffed-up chests, sweaty brows, and lots of ideas about what things need to be done, but nary a one good idea about how to do them."

"You watch. One day." Solomon balled his fist and began

to box an invisible opponent. He jabbed twice and polished him off with a vicious uppercut. "One day."

A figure charged into Ledbetter's store, barreled over, but carefully so as not to drop a jar lodged in his hand. Horace. His tears from Monday had turned into a fit of laughter. "Who you fighting there, Solomon?" Horace asked. "Can't take on no real man, so you gots to beat up on the air." He laughed and took a swig from his jar.

Ledbetter scolded Horace for drinking inside the store. "You know my rules: take it out back! Stupid nigger done spent what little money he got on corn liquor and he's drunk already." Ledbetter turned to Solomon and whipped his splayed hand in Horace's direction. "Now here's the new Negro for you. Good luck on accomplishing anything of significance with the likes of this one in your ranks."

Horace pointed at Ledbetter and as more laughter erupted, snot spurted from his nose, and a snub cigar fell from the corner of his mouth. "Your proper talk is funny Mr. Ledbetter! Sometimes you be more white than the white man hisself."

Solomon joined in with the laughter and helped straighten Horace up. "Come on. Let me get you home, buddy."

Horace wrapped his heavy arm around Solomon's shoulder. Solomon clutched Horace's waist tightly. The evening sun shone like a beacon through the doorway and the two headed out.

"I'm going to miss that bread, Solomon," Horace said. His laughter dripped into a pool of solemnity on the gravelly roadway outside of Ledbetter's store. "Right when it's fresh in the morning, one of the oven gals would sneak me a loaf. It'd be so warm and soft, you want to cuddle with it like a baby child. I'd eat off it all day long. Every day for three years."

"Well, if that's the only thing you going to miss about Kimball's then you'll be alright. You've got people over at the cotton mill; you can find work over there."

A scowl grew across Horace's face. "I know there's mill work, but hell's bells if I ever thought I would end up there again."

Solomon knew mill work, too. At least what he had heard from the workers during their day's-end litanies unleashed at Ledbetter's. They talked about the gruel of hard labor in loud closed-in spaces, dust-ridden air that made it hard to breathe, bodacious boll weevils, and oppressive cracker foremen who'd never gotten notice of Lincoln's proclamation.

"How about I talk to Kimball, convince him of giving you your job back?"

"No convincing Kimball of anything, you know that, Sol."

Solomon shook his head, causing his lips to graze the side of Horace's face. Horace's black cheek felt tough, crusty— like the skin of a man thirty years older.

"Give me a taste of that corn," Solomon whispered.

Horace's limp arm swung the Mason jar up to Solomon's nose. An acrid vapor foretold the potency of the clear liquid, which eddied around the bottom half of the jar. Solomon held air in his nose and took a swift shot. A sweet pinch numbed his tongue and then a soft fullness slowly drained into his system.

"Stuff got a nice kick to it, don't it?" Horace teased. "But then your mouth get used to it and your tongue let you take it down nice and slow. And when it's sliding down your

16

throat, it feel so warm and good to you. That's the way I take on things in life, Solomon. That's why this Kimball thing won't get to me. It stang real bad at first. But now that I'm taking it all in, it ain't so bad."

"But you ain't got no job, Horace, and you won't have one tomorrow."

"But tonight, I feel good, Solomon."

Back and forth between the two the corn liquor swung like a happy pendulum, until Solomon downed the last drop and threw the jar into a distant brush. Slouched and arm-in-arm, they walked a slow two-step, their bodies balanced only by the weight of each other.

"Where can we get some more of this stuff, Horace?"

Horace's eyes sobered for a second. "You sure you want some more?"

"To hell with it. You're right, for once in your life, Horace," Solomon said. "Tonight, for one night only, let's feel good."

"You paying?"

Solomon stopped and wiggled his thigh. The loose change in his pocket jingled.

Miss Thelma's barking mutt guided their ears to her 9th Street yard, cluttered with rusted automobile parts that served no purpose other than to make it more difficult to access her front door. Once there, Solomon knocked three times, real hard. A little child's voice offered a stern, two-word instruction: "Round back."

Standing hunched over at the back doorway of her screen porch in a housecoat, snaggletooth Miss Thelma railed against stupid drunk niggers banging on her front door after she specifically spread the word all throughout

The Terry for them not to. She counted the change Solomon had emptied into her hand then nodded, inside, at a bouncy little girl with half-tended-to hair.

The girl brought over two glistening jars. "Here you go, Grand," she said.

"Thank you, Miss Thelma," Horace offered meekly. The screen door slammed shut, and with a clenched fist, Miss Thelma ordered her paying customers off the property. Horace screwed open his jar and took a gulp of the liquid.

"Hold on there, mister, we got the whole night ahead of us. Let's get to somewhere safe."

"You right."

Solomon retrieved the jars and slid them into his oversized pant pockets. Providing balancing weight to his high-flying head, the jars seemed to make walking easier. He led the night stroll all the way to the back dock at Kimball's Bakery, where the delivery trucks were parked in congruent angles, asleep for the night.

"Let's go to your old truck," Solomon said.

Horace jimmied open the rear door and scoped the empty bed of what had been his work home for years. The two found and settled into spots amidst the wooden crates. Solomon produced the jars of corn liquor like nuggets of gold. Eager laughter escaped from Horace, who took his jar and immediately took a taste. "A toast, to this old gal," Horace said, pounding a fist on the bed of the truck. "I'm going to miss her."

"It's steel and rubber, Horace. Don't go get all sentimental on me."

"If you didn't want me to get sentimenty on you, then why you bring me back here? To the scene of the crime?"

"Excellent choice of words there, buddy. A crime was committed on you, Horace, by Kimball, and now we are going to exact some justice."

Horace's confused eyes flickered and Solomon's searching eyes darted around the truck. Solomon smiled, reached for his pants pocket, and ripped it clean off.

"What's gotten into you, Sol?"

Solomon didn't answer and hopped out of the truck bed. Horace peered around the corner of the rear door and watched as Solomon opened the truck's fuel cap, swirled the piece of denim around its edges, then dipped it into the filler neck of the gasoline line as far as it would go.

"What you doing there, Sol?"

Solomon didn't answer. He got back into the truck, broke off a stake from one of the wooden crates, then violently poked a hole in the cap of the corn liquor jar. He cursed a splinter that pierced his palm.

"Give me one of them cigars you got, why don't you," he said. He twisted the gasoline-doused denim around the cigar and secured his makeshift wick into the hole made in the jar cap. "Horace, how much do you hate that bastard Kimball? All the things he's ever done to you. How much you want to make him pay?"

"I don't know. Solomon," Horace answered in a whisper.

Solomon lit a match. The flame glinted, illuminating Horace's sweaty dark skin.

"You ready?"

"Ready for what, Solomon?"

"Ready to run like you just seen the Klan? On the count of three?"

Solomon didn't wait for an answer. He started his

countdown, put fire to wick, and flung the jar into a window of the old Kimball house. The jar crashed a windowpane, and shattered after hitting the floor inside. Solomon then led Horace on a Jesse Owens dash to bushes across the street. They hunched down, eyes focused on the old house. Its rotting insides should have been the ideal kindling, but a minute ticked by and nothing happened. Solomon emerged from the bushes disappointed, hands on hips, marching in a spiral of frustration. As he stood there in the middle of the street, a streak of flames clinging to the edges of a curtain burst from the window, then to the sill, alongside the shutters and upwards towards the roof. Solomon let loose a great whelp, raised his hands victoriously and joyfully skipped back towards the bushes and a crouching Horace.

"What in God's name have you done?" Horace said, his bloodshot eyes open wide as they could be.

"*We've* done it, Horace. We've just got us some get back."

With persistence, the flames began to blacken the sides of the main bakery building, Kimball's mortgaged industrial trophy.

A siren roared from the distance, forcing Solomon and Horace to retreat further back into the density of the bushes, but still close enough to maintain a keyhole view at the burning building. After the fire trucks arrived to the scene, a gathering of neighbors huddled around. The firemen jostled through, secured a hose, and aimed a stream of water towards the center of the old house.

"Smell that," Horace said, noisily taking in a whiff of air. "Look like that fire got ahold to the day-old crates. Smell like toast."

"Some jam would go good, maybe some molasses," Solomon teased. He laughed and finished off the remains of Miss Thelma's liquor. "Can't wait to see little Kimball's face tomorrow," he said, though he wouldn't have to wait long. Kimball showed up minutes later in a nightshirt tucked into dress pants. Casually he strolled and paced in the street, ignoring the consoling gestures of neighbors and the concern of firefighters and police officers who'd no doubt grown up on Kimball's bread themselves. Kimball was smoking a pipe as his business went up in flames.

Horace pointed a thumb at the scene—the charred skeleton of the old house, the burning dock of the main building, and the thick black smoke disappearing into the night sky. "That's some spectacle we caused over there, Solomon. You right. I do feel better." Horace then released another blaring laugh and joked again about the kinds of jams the odor of burning bread had him hungry for. "Strawberry would be good, or peach. I love peach. Oh, apricot. Some apricot would be nice, too. How about you, Sol, what kind of jam would you want?"

"Oh, I don't know. Peach maybe." Solomon began to laugh along with Horace, their drunken giggles propelling to a rhythmic call and response. The fire had spread to the parked trucks. Solomon's, the one he drove for nearly ten years, caught the first flames. He reached into his pocket, attempting to count by feel the remaining coins he had on his possession. Not much was there and not much more was secured at home. Watching his truck engulfed by fire, Solomon realized that he too would be out of a job the next day. His laughter, it stopped.

Assisted Living

They all had these grandkids they liked to talk about all the time. Grown ones living in faraway cities, enjoying impressive lives and doing very important things like being lawyers and doctors and pharmacists or, in the case of the little bald-headed lady, an executive producer all the way out in Los Angeles. She never told anybody exactly what her grandson the executive producer really made out in L.A. TV shows? Movies? Just went around saying that he had climbed to the top and distinguished himself from lowlife regular producers. The others just smiled; they didn't know what the hell an executive producer did. The conversations would happen at about the same time every day, just minutes after I would arrive. The only thing that worked like clockwork at the Blair Assisted Living Home: the grandkids conversation.

Mrs. Bernice Hobbs was my charge—that's the word all the caregivers used—for two hours a day, three days a week, all because, on a dare, I messed around with a couple of dudes on the football team. I didn't do nothing. Not really. They never even took their underwear off. I had no intentions of letting anything crazy happen, putting my name out there so somebody could add me to their list of sluts at school. But in a brief moment of what my daddy called rebellious insanity, I ditched Mrs. Rockwell's boring-as-hell third period *Consumer Economics* class—where she spends way too much time explaining the simplest of things like "how to open a bank account"— and joined them fools behind the auditorium stage. A minute later that gorilla-faced vice principal Mr. Dandridge came making his clean sweep on the first floor. He tries to fool students, creeping up on the same spots twice sometimes within a few minutes. He did just that the one Thursday I decided to be stupid, right when the school choir was out front practicing a gospel song, singing all off-key and way too loud.

More concerned with why we weren't in class than what it must have looked like we were doing, Mr. Dandridge shook his head as he came stomping over, yelling up a storm with his crooked pointing finger stabbing the air all around himself. Dandridge rounded us up like cattle—me, Derrick Banks, Tre Wallace, and LaShon Merritt—and herded us down the hall to the guardhouse, which is what everyone called his stank one-window office. I sat in the chair behind Dandridge's desk. He made the three boys sit on this ratty faux-leather sofa he had on the opposite side of his office, lest we try anymore "funny business" while he went about completing his hallway surveillance. We sat there the rest of the period staring at the bare, puke-green cinderblock walls. Mr. Dandridge came back in, empty-handed but smelling foul as a chimney. He didn't catch anybody else. Apparently he just sneaked out for a smoke, probably under the teachers' favorite big oak tree in the school's front lawn. He motioned for me to get out his chair, told us to refresh his memory and tell him what our names were.

We stared at each other, splitting amongst ourselves that

damned fool look people give when they feel really, *really* stupid. We could have been out of that office and Old Black Dandridge wouldn't have known where to begin to find us because he didn't even know our names. Or maybe he did and he was playing games with us again. He was slick. I reminded myself that we did get caught in the first place. If we had snuck out, we would have been in worse trouble than we already were. We did the right thing by deciding to stay right there in the office. Not that we even considered the notion of escaping. The four of us had stayed just about completely silent the whole time. Tre did whisper one thing, but like the experienced detention hall regulars they were, Derrick and LaShon told him to keep his mouth shut. *"Don't volunteer no information. Answer everything either 'yes' or 'no.' That's it."* Yeah, those three were headed straight to the penitentiary. How stupid was I for messing with them?

We gave Dandridge our names as we had learned to do freshman year: last name, first name, spelling it out, especially if your mama and daddy made up something complicated with all kinds of combinations of vowels and consonants and apostrophes.

"Riggs, Yvonne, Y-V-O-N-N-E." I stood over him as he tapped out our names on his computer to see how many strikes we had against us.

Dandridge moused his way down a list displaying on his computer screen. *Strikes* actually appeared as tiny little check marks. *Major Infraction Disciplinary Demerit* a pop-up screen would helpfully explain each time Dandridge paused over one of the little check marks. He got to my name. I had two. The first strike I got after slapping some trick on the bus who bumped into me and made me drop a ten-pound chemistry book on my foot. Strike two came after I told Ms. Beasley I had been late to her music class because, well, I wanted to be. She first put her hands out all apologetically and told me, "Yvonne, it's not that you're not doing your work, it's just that you've got a nasty attitude." I didn't say nothing, thinking that maybe she would just go on about her business and tell me to just sit down. Instead, she wrote me up and pointed me to the main office where this little ghetto fab administrative assistant who wore velour suits to work made a few clicks with her mouse and gave me another strike, one short of a mandatory twelve-day suspension, which could like seriously fuck you up if you were college-bound like me.

"I can't get no strike three, Mr. Dandridge!"

He scrolled through my records and saw some pretty good grades. Then, like out of nowhere, a mean frown grew over his ugly face, like he was a movie monster ready for attack. His big red lips then smacked all chimpanzee-like as he said, "Well, you should have thought of that before you cut class and decided to go off and have a picnic behind the stage. You kids need to learn there are consequences to your actions."

A *picnic?* Is that what he thought was going on? Man was straight out of his right mind. So he dismissed the boys, all those fools amazingly just on strike two. They smiled and giggled that silly thug cackle, covering their mouths like they didn't want nobody to smell their breath, slouching over like they had no spines and bouncing off each other like wobbly bowling pins.

I prayed a little prayer, hoping those boys would not go mouthing off, spreading rumors about me, exaggerating what had happened. At least Tre, the pretty one, had the decency to convey an apology with sad clown eyes and a twisted up mouth.

I turned back to Dandridge. "Please, can we work something out? I can't get no third strike. I'm doing good in Algebra II right now. Strike three would literally kill me."

"Believe me, Ms. Riggs, it won't *literally* kill you." Mr. Dandridge tapped on his keyboard again. He liked the power he had on those keys. He tapped on them real hard and quick. "So, you're taking Algebra II from Mrs. Brannen this semester?"

Didn't I just say that, you Alzheimer's-having fool?

"Yes, sir, and I'm pulling a B+," I told him.

He started yammering about consequences and actions again, and some other nonsense he himself must have been tired of hearing coming out of his mouth. Then out of the blue, a fire alarm buzzed and saved me. Probably pulled by one of the three Neanderthals who had just left. Mr. Dandridge said he would deal with me later. He dusted off his suit sleeve and went off to the races to track down the alarm culprits.

Two phone calls to my parents and three school days later, I learned that Dandridge had turned my case over to the principal, Dr. Hobbs. This was a good thing. A very good thing. Dr. Hobbs had been my family's across-the-street neighbor for over ten years. He and his wife were friendly with my folks, though we were a little jealous that his house was bigger than ours. He didn't like to mention our neighborhood connection at school though, never swerving our hallway conversations into neighborly chitchat.

Dr. Hobbs's assistant summoned me to his office first

thing that next Friday morning. He had decorated his office way nicer than Dandridge did his. Dr. Hobbs had real class and taste. He even dressed nice; sharp suits, classy patterned ties. He made me wait across from his desk as he read some paperwork, responded to emails, made a phone call, and gave the morning announcements, complete with a "thought of the day" at the end. I got mad about the waiting, but couldn't stay too angry at a man who had enough self-pride and dignity to fix up a nice workspace for himself.

When he got to me, Dr. Hobbs let out a big sigh and started fingering over his thick mustache and playing a little drumbeat on his pouting bottom lip. "I've talked it over with your parents, Yvonne, and we all agreed that a strike three and a suspension will serve no valuable rehabilitative purpose. So, we have something more creative in mind. Not a punishment, per se, but an experience that will provide you with opportunities for sober reflections on life and its responsibilities. Perhaps raise up some of the sensitivity that we know is beneath the surface of all this rebellious behavior."

And *boom*—just like that, I had this mandatory volunteer job spending time with Dr. Hobbs's mother at an old folks' home. That neighbor connection thing saved me, proved to have some value, or so I thought.

She smelled a little like pee. My first day there, I sat in the one hard wooden chair they put in each resident's room for their visitors. I asked Mrs. Hobbs in a loud voice if she needed for me to do anything. She just sat in her leather chair as we watched afternoon shows on TV. After around like the seventh visit, I asked what I could do for her. She quietly told me to find a brush that was in her top dresser drawer. I brushed her hair and even tried to style it a little bit. She had nice hair for an old lady, real thick and nice to touch. The next couple of weeks we got into a routine of hair brushing, talk shows and just sitting. Being locked up in that room forced me to start in on my homework right away each day. I pulled my B+ to a low A in Algebra II. After a month, when the weather turned nicer, I would escort Mrs. Hobbs into the sunny common area which had a bunch of old TVs always playing the same channel. There she got to spend time with all the others and listen to them ramble on about what was on their minds, like grandchildren who never came to visit. She started to like this part of my day a little too much and wanted me to take her out there as soon I got to work, so every day we'd end up in the common area; me, Mrs. Hobbs and a bunch of old people talking about their grown grandchildren.

It seemed as if they all became my charges. The caregivers at the home who were actually getting paid to attend to the residents loved that; they could spend that much more time talking on their phones or to each other about their bad kids or cheating boyfriends and no-good husbands. Nobody really ever introduced me to the residents; Mrs. Hobbs didn't really know any of them by name. I gave them pretend nicknames so I could remember who was who. The first ones were kind of mean—*Mr. Doesn't Wipe Himself* or *Sally One Tooth*, stuff like that. But you can't let the mean stuff stay in your head too long. Maybe that's what Dr. Hobbs meant about some sober responsibilities teaching a person life lessons and whatnot. I eventually learned their real names from the staff, who were instructed to call the residents *Mr. This* and *Mrs. That*. So at 3:30 p.m. sharp, I'd walk Mrs. Hobbs into the common room and greet all the residents who had come by for afternoon entertainment and a piece of sunlight.

"I've never been called 'mister' so much in my life," Mr. Harley told me. Each day, he'd reveal a little more about his life. He fought in Vietnam during the early years. Over there they just called him *Harley*. After the war, he moved to Gary, Indiana, and worked in a factory where the bosses called him every name in the book, but definitely never mister. He retired and moved back South to take care of his ailing mother. People then began to know him as *Miss Harley's boy*, except on Sunday, when it was *Deacon* Harley.

"Mama passed on twenty years ago," Mr. Harley told me. "Life has just sailed by since. I'm turning the corner around seventy-three, and finally I'm my own fulltime *mister*." Mr. Harley reached for my hand after he said that. Mrs. Hobbs cut her eyes and seemed jealous, so I reached for hers too. The three of us held hands for almost an hour and listened to one of them judge shows blasting on all the TVs.

In the mornings before classes, I began stopping by Dr. Hobbs's office occasionally to tell him how the previous day with his mother went. When I passed Mr. Dandridge in the hall, you could just tell my special arrangement made him mad as hell. He'd smack those lips then make all kinds of grunt sounds at me. I should have gotten suspended, to be an example. What's the use of having a *three strikes and you're out* policy if the rules weren't going to be followed? I wanted to stick my tongue out and tease him. Of course, I couldn't go that far, but when I knew Dandridge was standing within earshot, I did talk especially loud to Dr. Hobbs, filling in the pauses of our conversations with my silly laugh, making it sound like we were the best of friends. I knew that had to make Dandridge so pissed.

A few days before the semester was to end, I stopped by

Dr. Hobbs's office again. "Mother's spirits seemed to really be lifted by your presence, Yvonne." He used a voice I'd never heard come from him before. He sounded astonished. Happy. Relieved. All at once. Not at all like a tired old principal is supposed to sound. "She couldn't stop talking about the puzzle game you've got everyone at Blair addicted to now. What's it called? *Sukiyaki?*"

I laughed a little. "*Sudoku,* Dr. Hobbs. Mrs. Brannen makes us do them before she begins class. She said Sudoku exercises your brain waves, gets them flowing, helps you to concentrate and keep you focused. Much better than popping Ritalin, she says. I figured if it is good for that, then Sudoku might fend off Alzheimer's. Not that I'm a doctor or anything."

Dr. Hobbs got all reflective on me and stroked his chin. I wondered if I offended him or scared him a little. Got him thinking about his mother maybe one day losing it completely and what that must be like. I tried to reassure him that though Mrs. Hobbs stayed quiet and distant at times, she came nowhere near close to the legitimate Alzheimer's I had seen firsthand at Blair. It's hellish to see up close and personal. Your eyes see an old person, perhaps full of life experience, wisdom, and knowledge, but your ears hear a child who don't even know what day of the week it is. It's the saddest of things.

"Well, the agreement was just through the end of the semester, Ms. Riggs. You see this through the week after exams and your record will be totally clean going into your senior year."

Dr. Hobbs dismissed me to my music class, but my mind had already gone back to Blair. I felt good about doing something good. I felt good about making Dr. Hobbs feel good about his mother.

During exams, I studied hard and killed those tests, thanking my lucky stars that I had the opportunity to take them. I walked out thinking I had a chance at making A's across the board, which made me really scared about what could have been if I had gotten strike three. All those potential A's wouldn't exist; some college admissions person would see a report card full of F's with no explanation about stupid disciplinary demerits and how some old white man school board member who liked baseball decided to make a three strikes rule. There'd be no footnotes or character witnesses. No one would be looking over their shoulders to shout about the good grades that were in my record. I'd probably have to go to community college, waitress tables for a year, or maybe not do anything at all. Thinking about it made me nervous, filled my whole body with shakes. I heard Dandridge's gravelly voice in my head singing "Actions. Consequences. Actions. Consequences." I wanted to punch him dead in his nose for being able to get inside my mind like that.

So, my last day at Blair turned out be Mrs. Hobbs's last day too. Mr. Hobbs was going to move his mother into his house, right across the street from us. Said Blair was no place for a person who still had life in them to live out their days. The late spring heat had ended our visits to the sunny common area. We spent that last afternoon in her room, which had been chilled to the bone by a window unit air-conditioner. We fussed a bit over the temperature setting—what old person doesn't get too cold?—but with so many residents stopping by to visit Mrs. Hobbs by then, the space would quickly warm with their body heat and slow, familiar conversations. Mr. Harley came by and repeated the same story of the time he saw a man get shot on the streets of Gary. "Scared you back South, did it?" Mrs. Hobbs and I said almost at the exact same time, finishing the story for him. We all laughed together.

When 5:30 p.m. rolled around, two new faces from the staff came to see Mrs. Hobbs off. When it came to employees, Blair had worse turnover than the cafeteria at school.

"Looks like you're going to be leaving us, Mrs. Hobbs. We certainly enjoyed your stay!" one of them said. She had to read Mrs. Hobbs's name off a piece of paper on her clipboard and talked in a high-pitched voice as if she were trying to calm down a fussy three-year-old. That made me mad. But then the second one had to go and whisper, "I suspect it's not too often we're going to see them checking out upright." That made me madder. She stood right next to me. I know she knew I heard her. Dr. Hobbs didn't though, and I was glad for that. He draped a sweater over his mother and guided her out the door, confident that he could take care of her better at his home.

"And who are you, young lady?" the first caregiver asked me, after ignoring me the whole time like I wasn't even in the room.

Mrs. Hobbs, feeling cheerful and relieved as hell to be on the other side of that doorway, looked over her shoulder and smiled at them. "That's my granddaughter," she said. She winked at me, and I grabbed her tiny hand tight as I could.

The Benefactress

(1927)

It had been such a long ride. Will dusted off his rumpled suit jacket, wondering how it had gotten so soiled on the train. From the seats, he concluded. The railway people seldom bothered to put forth any effort to truly clean the colored sections, and Will made the mistake of sitting on the jacket just past the North Carolina state line. He damned his carelessness, but quickly unflustered his mind, knowing the situation had to be addressed before the day's meeting with Mrs. Deal.

His options? A quick stopover at Cousin Marietta's in Harlem. He could get the jacket—and himself—spruced up there. A visit to Marietta's would not end quickly, though. She'd just moved up North a few years before and, though she'd never let loose an admission, was sick for home. When Will visited last, she peppered him with silly questions about Georgia, as if it had been a century since she'd set foot in her homeland.

"Yes, Marietta," Will had answered repeatedly, before having to recount the details of the memories warmed over in her mind—the sweetest of peaches, the reddest red clay, and the aroma of old ladies' kitchens filling the streets with smoky goodness. However, to trump any notion of happy times down South, Marietta offered litanies about the wonders of Harlem's people, its businessmen, a dignified high society, an earnest laboring class, and all the handsome bachelors who'd come back from the Great War readying their people for *something*, something entirely new. Even the criminals of Harlem were different, she'd maintained. Happy-go-lucky they were, not at all malicious or bloated with pure evil and hatred like their daring and foolish Southern brothers.

"It's a whole 'nother world, Will," she'd said before tsk-tsking his decision to remain in Dixie and take the position to head a colored high school. "What possessed you?" she had asked, answering herself with a recurrent refrain: "Lord only knows."

Exactly, Will thought. Although he hadn't become the minister he'd trained to be at the seminary, a missionary's zeal burned within and led him to the school. How and why, Lord only knew.

But the detail he detested most was upon him, requiring an exhaustive train trip all the way to New York City, then an automobile journey to the center of Long Island, and finally a session with Mrs. Deal. The first time had been such an adventure. The glimpses of the soaring skylines in the Northern cities. The purposeful bustle of people with white faces so different than those in the South, some with darker-hued complexions, different-shaped features. But the yearly travel had grown wearisome, even as the contributions grew. Will reached for the last of his headache powders to prepare himself for the day's work ahead.

"Professor, is that you?" Will heard a familiar voice, rising above the sounds of conversation chatter and brisk footsteps echoing within the train hall. It was Mrs. Deal's driver, Blue, a lean, dark-complexioned fellow who'd known nothing but the North and the city his entire young life. He spotted Will's problem right away.

"I know where we can get that coat cleaned up," he said. His nodding head indicated the kind of confidence often found in Northern-bred colored people, a tame condescension Will learned to tolerate with a Bible in hand.

"But Mrs. Deal specifically set the meeting at two-thirty in the afternoon. Let's not get the both of us in trouble, Blue. It'll be okay. I just need to dust off, here." Will attempted to beat the coat with the palms of his hands. It only seemed to spread more dust over the charcoal gray wool fabric.

"Trust me, Professor, with that old Mrs. Deal, you're better off being a little tardy with a clean jacket and shined-up face than being early and looking like some ashy, country field nigger straight from a tobacco farm down South."

"Is it that bad?"

Blue nodded. In his crisp fall uniform—black with starched whiteness peeking around his neck and wrists—he reached for Will's bag and showed him to the car.

In Mrs. Deal's automobile, Blue drove Will through Manhattan streets crowded with commuting working men who had already started their days. Will marveled at how ordinary he seemed to appear to them, how they did not take special notice of him and his colored driver deftly navigating the city's grid and its mid-morning traffic. Back home, the sight would elicit disapproving glances and perhaps dramatic hysterics from onlookers: 'Look at that uppity nigger with his nigger driver!' In New York, Will saw only disinterested head turns. As always, it was the nicest part of the trip; an opportunity to enjoy the anonymity and pretense of a chauffeured ride in the big city. The car passed the point where the double-digit-numbered streets turned into triple-digit-numbered streets. As Blue drove on, the surroundings grew more familiar to Will and the faces of the sidewalk pedestrians had become darker.

"Just where are we going, Blue?" Will asked. "If we're heading this far uptown, we might as well call on my cousin Marietta."

"No, sir," Blue said. "My way will be quick and easy. No tears and prayers, and no one making a fuss over you and all. No smiles about old times or peach pie."

Blue had remembered the stories about long visits with Marietta. Mrs. Deal liked such attention to detail. It was one of the reasons she'd taken Blue on as her driver—a brief layover on the journey to do great things for his people, she once said, after he'd outgrown his youthful stubbornness or taken classes at the City College like she'd urged.

Blue circled the car around a block then waved to a smiling shopkeeper who recognized the car before he could surely see Blue's face. He parked in front of a soot-covered walkup building sandwiched tightly in a long row of others. A woman appeared in the doorway and Blue explained the reason for his visit. She immediately assessed the damage to the suit jacket and invited Blue and Will upstairs to her spare but well-appointed room.

"I'll spot-clean it and iron out the wrinkles. We shall have you looking good as new, Professor," the woman said before introducing herself as Blue's mother. "Have some tea, Professor. It will relax your vocals so you'll be ready for the session, and all those intelligent-sounding words God has filled your head with will flow easily so you can get your money to educate our children who so desperately need improvement."

Will put his mouth to Blue's ear, his lips grazing a lobe. "Your mother seems to know quite a bit about my business here in New York," he whispered.

Blue lit the stove and put an old iron kettle on top of one of the burners. Whispering back, he said, "Professor, you been coming this way for all these years I've worked for Mrs. Deal, and even some more years before that. You would expect that it would come up in routine conversations along the way, now wouldn't you?"

"I'm not scolding you, son. It's just that Mrs. Deal, I'm sure, likes to keep her private business and goings-on private."

"Professor, it's not like I'm writing you up in the newspapers, and there's positively no chance that Mother will ever engage with Mrs. Deal socially. And besides, Mrs. Deal do like for *certain* folks to know about all the money she gives to them colored schools down South. Why you think she makes such a do with the sessions? Like she couldn't just send a bank check or wire the money at her leisure after she's read one of those fine letters you send to her, telling her how well things are going for the school."

It was rare for Blue to speak negatively about Mrs. Deal. Will took this talk as a sign of trust. He decided, in that moment, he liked Blue even more than he previously thought. The Northern coloreds were in an enviable spot. Able to think more freely, broadly and clearly about the world they navigated.

The kettle whistled, agitating Will's aching head just as

the train's whistle had done during the trip. Blue took the kettle from the stove and poured the steaming water into a pot filled with dried leaves and an assortment of spices. "It's Ma's own blend. Should remind you of home. She says it's a Carolina recipe." The tea smelled of mint and ginger and sassafras to Will. He drank it slowly as Blue looked on.

"All ready," Blue's mother announced from the adjoining room. She held up the suit jacket for inspection, eyeing the smoothed-out fabric up and down, then down and up.

"That's perfect, Ma," Blue said. "Let's get to going, Professor."

Will thanked Blue's mother profusely and apologized for extending her day of washing and ironing. He reached for coins in his pants pocket. She refused him before he could offer any compensation.

"No, no, Professor," she said. "You keep what you would give me and put it up for your children. The work you're doing is so important for our people." She clasped her hands as if in prayer.

Blue ushered Will from the apartment. "What all have you told your mother about me, son?" Will asked.

"Shhh. No time, Professor. Time's a wasting. We don't want to be too late for old Mrs. Deal."

—

The city and its symphony of noises and odors had long faded into the background as Blue headed into more serene environs, finally reaching Mrs. Deal's town on Long Island after an hour's drive. Her home, with twin gables resembling eyes, overlooked the street like a diligent watchman. Will could see Mrs. Deal's shadowy hunched figure doddering about in one of the windows.

"Oh, she's looking out, Professor!" Blue said. He sped up and managed a giggle.

"Damn you, Blue. I know she is going to be upset!"

"Don't worry none," Blue said. He parked the car in a circular driveway a few feet from the front door. Blue entered the house with Will at his side. His voice rose as he started in on some talk about the terribly unreliable trains and the chaos of morning commotion in the city due to a horrid auto accident on 57th caused by an unskilled female driver.

"Lord, they surely need to not allow no fast young gals to get behind the steering wheel of a powerful machine such as an automobile!" Blue said. "Ought to be a law against it, wouldn't you say, Professor?"

Mrs. Deal emerged from the house's center stairway and down into the foyer. She lifted her spectacles to the bridge of her nose, nodded at Will, and motioned for him to have a seat in the parlor. She'd aged none since he first met her all those years ago. And even in the photographs Will had seen of her as a young woman, she looked to be a sturdy, not-quite-old old woman.

"What took so long, Blue?" Mrs. Deal said finally. "You should have been here an hour ago."

Blue started up his tale again. "Horrible accident, Mrs. Deal, you should have seen it! These gal drivers are causing havoc all over the nation! There ought to be a law. I tell you, Mrs. Deal."

"Oh, don't tell me anything," Mrs. Deal said. "Go on with your excuses, Blue!" She shooed him out the front door, closing it behind his snickering.

"He's got much potential, but will have to grow out of his childishness to reach it," Mrs. Deal said, securing herself in a grand chair in the parlor. A tea set was set out on a side table. Will had come to know the china during the visits, one odd-colored cup always reserved for him. "Now, tell me all about the accomplishments of the year. I'm eager to hear of what the children are learning." Mrs. Deal wanted to know right away about the returns she was getting on her investment in the Eastern Georgia Normal, Agricultural, and Industrial School for Colored Children.

Will inhaled. He had planned to begin the conversation by highlighting the rousing reception the school's choir had received on its tour of Presbyterian churches in South Carolina, or how his shop classes had become so accomplished that they were taking furniture orders from local citizens, both colored and white.

"We've had a very productive year, Mrs. Deal," Will began. He decided to talk first about the choir, which had taken upon itself to learn and perform a particularly challenging Russian choral work.

Mrs. Deal nodded. She reached for a large leather album, a grandiose checkbook. She opened it to a page of three conjoined blank checks.

"You know, the choir at the Manassas Colored School in Virginia sang the very same work before the King of Sweden at an embassy affair in Washington, D.C. this year. It was very well received. At least this is what I've heard."

Will's lip tightened. He should have known she'd bring up the Manassas School choir. "Yes, I do remember reading something about that in one of the colored weeklies. Quite an operation Miss Fennel has down in Manassas. We correspond periodically to exchange ideas. I admire her work and tenacity much."

"Indeed," Mrs. Deal said. "It made all the newspapers. I've been considering doubling my involvement there this year." She removed a blank check and carefully rested it atop her book. "Hand me my pen, will you, W.L.?" she asked, not looking away from the check. "And continue, please. Tell me more."

"Our shop students are doing marvelous woodwork and carpentry. They've earned themselves quite a reputation around town. They're turning out chairs and tables and even dressers. Their work is very polished and elegant," Will said. "You could sell it in the finest of furniture stores in Manhattan." He reached for Mrs. Deal's pen and inkwell, which were resting on a nearby desk. "They will be prepared well for careers in woodworking or carpentry. In fact, I've got a small token that a student in the first-year class made especially for you." Will had almost forgotten about the napkin rings wrapped in handkerchiefs in his bag. He pulled them out and held them up for Mrs. Deal's inspection. The rings were polished to a gleaming auburn color, and her initials were inscribed inside. A smile spread over Mrs. Deal's face, the first one of the afternoon. With careful attention, she signed her name on the check. She'd learned calligraphy a half-century ago at Vassar, and her signature had always been an artful representation of herself: graceful, elegant, and winsome—all the things she wasn't physically. Will smiled as she completed the signature. It didn't take nearly as long as usual.

"Now tell me about this Latin instructor you've hired," Mrs. Deal asked. "Miss Fennel says you've hired a fine fellow, who'd been pursued by some of the Negro colleges."

Will had once taught Latin himself—as an elective during after-school instruction—until he found a qualified teacher to come lead a bona fide class. Passing through during a holiday, the teacher traded quips with Will at a family gathering. The fresh seminary graduate was weighing on his career options—'teacher or preacher?'—when Will convinced him to stay in town and teach beginner's Latin to his third- and fourth-year students, ones who had a real chance at attending college themselves. The lessons would cover just the basics truly: some foundational vocabulary work to spur them to seek deeper understanding of theology, the sciences, laws and governance. And to train their minds to be working participants in the pursuit of self-betterment. Just four seniors had taken the Latin class the previous year, so Will had the young teacher tutor others in religion and literature as well. Will had grown quite fond of the young man and the work he had done with his Latin students. He especially liked his studiousness and quiet pride, qualities he believed they shared.

"Seems quite the luxury, a full-time instructor for four pupils," Mrs. Deal offered, her head haughtily rocking backwards. "Now, W.L., do you think he's worth the expense?"

Will told of the teacher's fine credentials, his first-rate attitude, and the results he'd produced in one year: all of his senior students went on to enroll in seminaries and colleges. Their Latin instruction alone did not produce the result, obviously, but their minds had been ignited, their ambitions deepened.

He called the teacher by the nickname he'd been given by the students—Little Lee Roy—and described his petite build, handsome features, and fair complexion, so Mrs. Deal could conjure up a pleasant image to counter her misgivings. He told her of his fine family background. Father: lecturer of literature and arts at Lincoln University; mother: a dabbler in opera singing and a descendant of a notable Philadelphia freedman. He told her about the easygoing nature Little Lee Roy had with white people in town, who'd grown to respect his professorial demeanor and how his very presence bettered relationships between the races.

"If he's as remarkable as you make out, why is it only now that I hear of this young man? I had to get my information secondhand. You know I don't like that. It makes me think you're hiding things, W.L."

"To the contrary, Mrs. Deal. He's a young man of excellent character. I'd talk him up all day long given the opportunity. This was just an oversight in my correspondence, I assure you."

Mrs. Deal tucked the check back into her checkbook and went to a large bureau that sat in the corner of the room. She pulled open a draw overflowing with files, one labeled 'EGNAI.' From the file poured out several letters Will had written over the course of the year. There was something odd about seeing them all together—the same stationary all filled with Will's own words and his deliberate and steady penmanship. Instead of the friendly reports of the school's progress that they were, from the distance the letters looked to be official records being presented as court evidence.

"You keep those?" Will asked. He felt naked, exposed. Mrs. Deal return to her chair and thumbed through the page of the letters, painstakingly reading excerpts from each.

"Our students are enjoying their new civics texts immensely... We expect a bountiful garden of tomatoes and a bounty of cotton this year from our ag students, despite the relentless boll weevil... The children are taking wonderfully to their new athletics programs. Many are learning the game of basketball for the first time, thanks to the generous donation of equipment from your sporting goods friends..."

On and on she read from the stack until she reached the last one. She shuffled and aligned the letters on her lap.

"Not one mention about this Little Lee Roy Latin instructor fellow in any of them. And you speak so fondly of him now. I don't like this, Will. What good is it to take on this fellow if he's only going to teach four students—and Latin, of all things? We're trying to do practical things. You should have known better."

"I assure you, the long returns will be fruitful. If one of those four graduates becomes a teacher or becomes any sort of productive and contributing citizen, we have justified our investment."

Mrs. Deal paused reflectively as Will took one long sip of tea.

"We will give this instructor one month to find a new position," she said finally. You agree with that, W.L.?"

The order numbed Will, as it first rebounded against his chest and then gradually stole his will to disagree diplomatically. He'd had a hundred more reasons why Latin should remain a part of his curriculum, but none seemed more important than the check he had come for.

"If you think that is best."

"Don't worry about the young man," Mrs. Deal continued

with a charitable tone in her voice. "We'll find him a position. I will have a call put in to Miss Fennel at the Manassas School. She's building a fine pre-college program and will definitely have more use for him there. That is, if he is as fine as you say and willing to accept our offer."

Mrs. Deal filled out the check and tucked it into an envelope. Without words, she handed it to Will, who immediately dropped it in his bag.

"Now, tell me more about this fine furniture the children are crafting," she asked. As Will described the marvelous china closet his seventh graders were working to complete, Mrs. Deal drifted off to sleep. Still, he talked on, eager but hesitant to peek at the dollar amount on the check that his school would depend on for survival for another school year.

Love You, Always

He wasn't a *bad* father.

At one time or another, Lisa told that to boyfriends who were trying on sensitivity, girlfriends fishing for deep emotional connections, and at least one therapist who robotically read questions from a checklist. But how does one truly characterize a thirty-seven-year relationship, and the hundreds of thousands of moments entailed, as all bad or all good? How does one parse and tally up a man's life actions—those witnessed by other souls—so simply? He did some bad things, but not so bad when gauged against the worst of what you might see in TV movies or read about on the Internet daily. And he did some good things, but certainly nothing worthy of tear-soaked tributes and elegies.

His story began like many hesitant fathers: he seduced and won the prettiest girl in the neighborhood, Gloria, who would become Lisa's mother. He had *magnetism*, Gloria would say, as if she had a personal definition of the word others could not precisely understand. It was a mesmerizing attraction worthy of desiring, but one cloaked in echoing warning calls. However interpreted, he had it, charged by a smile that didn't soften toughness as it might have done to the less confident boys in the neighborhood. Leanness afforded his body a slithering gait, always rhythmically pacing ahead of a pack of envious followers and loyal hangers-on. And crowning the overall aesthetic, he played electric bass in a band, a real live funk machine, one supposedly not half-bad by high school standards. He liked to claim he started the group, teaching the others over time a style that put groove into the upbeats of pop melodies, a ploy to get both the black and white girls to like their music. But he reserved his wandering eyes for Gloria, the neighborhood white chick who sported gold hoop earrings, ample assets, and a caravan of black girlfriends who didn't mind that the most popular black boy on the block played in the snow. Eventually, Gloria *liked* him back. That magnetism was magic, Gloria confessed to her daughter in soft-spoken conversations played through reels of memories that unveiled a past equally worthy of teardrops, laughs, and sighs.

And so, there he was, Lisa's father George, nearly four decades removed from his teen love affair, his pretty face pockmarked with moles and marred by a mysterious winding scar, his lean body transformed to fast-food mush, his light eyes reddened and soulless, and his original and even secondary store-bought hair all but gone. There he was, trying to make amends to his only daughter. Again.

He leaned against the door of an old Cadillac, its paint dulled and chipping in spots. Standing in the doorway of her townhouse, Lisa waved him in, hoping to swiftly erase the scene of her father out front. Hoping to not have to later reveal to nosey neighbors the identity of the ridiculous grinning man in the purple jacket showing too much pride in a beat-up purple car.

"Looking like a million bucks! You'll always be my baby

girl," he said, trained to speak in lyrical iambic couplets—or, more likely, addicted to the rhythm of them.

Lisa extended her arms, inviting a hug to quickly lure him from the curb and into the house. As he approached and reached for the embrace, she re-familiarized herself with the smells: moth balls, smoke breath, and pungent cologne. Miraculously stale liquor seemed to evade him after all those years and just became his natural odor—so much so, Lisa didn't recognize it as a particular kind of liquor, just Daddy. Just George.

The prologues to these prodigal visits veered towards a roadside ditch filled with uncomfortableness. Lisa never knew exactly what to offer him or what to ask about. A set of rote questions repeated themselves over the years, and the answers meandered into nostalgia and regret and a bunch of emotional topics too heavy for once-a-year drop-ins, thus the yearly conclusion: He *was* a bad father, most of the time.

George eased himself to the dining room table, taking a seat at the head like it was his earned and rightful spot. Lisa sat at the opposite end, arms crossed and legs folded meditatively, this feat a recent accomplishment thanks to yoga classes and a post-pregnancy Mediterranean diet—nuts, grains, lean protein, and greens filled with nutrients to cleanse her body and soul.

"You really look good, baby girl, a proud mother and all, glowing the way you are," he said, raising clasped hands triumphantly, congratulating his contribution of DNA. Below one of those hands, a gaudy silver bracelet hung loosely around his wrist. On it, purple-encrusted stones spelled out something. Lisa squinted to see what exactly.

George slid his jacket sleeve up his arm a bit and struck a

hand model's pose. "You like this? 14 karat. White gold, not silver like everybody always seems to think. And those are pink diamonds. You don't see those every day, now do you?" He unclasped the bracelet, carefully spreading the trinket atop one of Lisa's plastic placemats before sliding the display across the table. Lisa stopped it with two hands, like a quick-reacting soccer goalie. She admired then fingered the pink diamond lettering. Indeed, one didn't see pink diamonds every day.

"L.Y.A.? Whose initials are those?" she asked.

"Not a who, but a what."

"Well, what is it?" Lisa halted herself before spilling an appended *Daddy*, which she did sometimes when hearing the word out loud felt comforting.

"*Love You. Always.* It means that."

"A gift to yourself? From yourself?"

"That's very funny, baby girl. No. A fan gave it to me, after a gig we had in Akron. They still appreciate the funk there. Ohio will always appreciate the funk."

Lisa tried on the bracelet. It slipped to the midpoint of her forearm. She gave it a whirl, spinning it like a little hula hoop around her wrist, showing the tacky thing all the respect it deserved. "Wait a minute. Fans? You all have those? Really? Still?"

"Don't be so mean, baby girl. It's not becoming. God didn't put women on this Earth to be mean. Your mother never had any of that in her soul, bless her." George would never say anything bad about his ex-wife. The true scoundrels never do, as they've learned the old trick of feigning humility and forgiveness. Lisa never fell for that shit.

"You want something to drink, George. Not liquor, I mean. I've got tea."

"That'll be nice," he said. "A little tea with my only child, all grown and sophisticated. Now that, I do remember. You having tea parties and playing with your tea sets. The smile on your face when holding court with imaginary playmates like you were the princess. The cute little English accent you used to do. You had pieces of a good regular childhood, even if you don't want to admit it."

Lisa exhaled, put the bracelet in her pocket, and went to the kitchen to fire up the tea kettle. George, planted at the table, wistfully began recounting the itinerary of the band's last tour. It had been a reunion of sorts that cobbled the remains of the original band members for performances in nightclubs and little venues in smaller cities—the kind of places where they appreciate you coming to them, he said.

The post-tour debriefing was familiar. During the period he lived with Gloria and Lisa, George would breeze through town at each month's end, excited to share what he had seen on the road— adoring fans, regular working people living good simple lives, the next big thing in music the label geniuses in New York and L.A. overlooked and ignored. Gloria and Lisa allowed such talk to drift aimlessly without response; he didn't seem to care if anyone actually listened anyway. His fairy tales, as Gloria called them, helped him to feel better in a place—his home—where he had a hard time feeling much of anything at all.

The weeks he was away, the arc of his career would be traced through stories in magazines—*Jet*, in those days—the playlists on AM soul stations, and lots of late-night phone calls from Willie, the band's manager, who strategically kept the guys copacetic by making sure the wives and girlfriends stayed equally and consistently informed. There were six of them, the *WAGs*. Gloria never bonded with the others, Hollywood girls who came on the scene after the band tasted a little success and the boys had cash money stuffing their pockets. And too, she didn't share the WAGs' fondness for all things long: hair, nails, winded conversations. But quietly, the women provided support and help when Lisa needed to be sent away from the fighting and the mood swings, when the eviction notice came, and finally when George just never returned after a tour. That occurred during Lisa's freshman year in high school, fortunately long after any peer would care about her tenuous connection to what passed for fame in places like Akron. He was never around anyway, so his extended absence didn't have to be explained. Another black dad MIA. Not exactly headline news.

Lisa returned to the table with the tea, unsweetened, unadorned, and served in coffee mugs that had been sitting unwashed in the sink. George sniffed and sipped, then tried to slip in another hug around Lisa's waist as she stood beside him. She inched away and took her own mug of tea back to the kitchen for sugar and a spot of milk.

"So, where did you really get this thing from?" she yelled over the hum of the refrigerator.

"Nothing to hide here, baby girl. I told you the truth."

Lisa stood in the kitchen doorway, swaying skeptically inside the frame and holding her mug. "It looks like it might actually be worth something. If you melted it down and sold the diamonds individually, not in its current gaudy incarnation. You may be running around with a little savings account on your arm, George. You'd better be careful. It might get stolen." She raised her eyebrows and cast a direct look at him. "Again."

"It's like I said. A fan gave it to me."

"And your 'fan' got it from?"

He didn't answer that, just went back to slurping tea and gazing around Lisa's townhouse, eyeballing and complimenting her things. ("You got pretty good taste. Just like your mama.") He wandered into the bedroom and gushed over the grandbaby he had not yet seen. Lisa followed behind him. He asked why she named him Lawrence, such a square-sounding name to have to live with for the rest of his life.

"It's his father's name. I wanted him to have something from his father that he could keep as his own, since things didn't work out between the two of us."

"I see," he said. "He'll grow into it. Maybe make it cool one day to be a Lawrence." George laughed. "Kind of the way me and ol' Clinton did with George." He reached for his grandson and guided him to his chest and into a gentle hug. As the baby rested on his suit lapel, George gruffly began singing an improvised lullaby. *"Little Lawrence, Little Lawrence, your mother thinks her father is a no-good thief, but little does she know that gives him no grief. 'Cause he's a good man, Little Lawrence, a good man you should know... just lived a life of love... loving too much. That's his only crime, Little Lawrence."*

Lisa didn't interrupt, thinking more so about forbidding herself from asking if he had a bed for the night. George would eventually let her know that he had arrangements and plans—a past-middle-aged man having to assert his independence should elicit some sympathy, so Lisa hugged him again, genuinely, on his way out. Fifteen minutes later, she swaddled Lawrence and headed to the one pawn shop that she knew still existed, one giving life to a dying strip mall in a past-depressed part of town.

"Love You. Always," she told the clerk, an older white woman with a round face and slits for eyes, probably wearied from appraising people's hopes for years and years.

"How much do you think it's worth?" Lisa asked.

"I will tell you, young lady, what I tell everyone who asks me that question—it's worth whatever someone is willing to pay for it. But with these initials on it, it may be worth a lot less than you're hoping for."

The clerk turned to a cluttered counter and examined the bracelet closely, hunching over as if to hide some secret examination techniques. She then tossed it atop a tiny scale with a digital display that ticked up to a final weight calculation. She swung back around and held the bracelet up to Lisa's face. "Three hundred dollars," the woman concluded matter-of-factly, impatiently so, as if a line of other customers were waiting to have their hopes dashed. In her head, Lisa inventoried the periodic Christmas and birthday gifts and one dollar bills tucked into surprise envelopes. All of that did not equal three hundred dollars for sure. This gift, he owed to her. If that was the best he could do then so be it.

"Honestly, miss, there's just too much crap jewelry out here and not much of a market for it anymore." The clerk laughed. "Nowhere to wear such fancy things these days. The men aren't taking us on the town like they used to, you know. Take it to one of these cash-for-gold places and be happy with whatever you get. Still though, I'll be willing to give you three hundred."

"Three hundred? That's all?" Lisa paused and looked at Lawrence for guidance. His sleeping eyes told her that if the jaded old pawnshop lady was thinking $300, then surely they could get triple that in the more legitimate marketplace;

perhaps online. Lisa grabbed the bracelet and left.

George called the next day, from a mobile number Lisa did not recognize. He'd found a bed to sleep in and someone who paid their cell phone bill to sleep with. He offered lunch.

"No need for that," she told him. "Things are as they have always been between us. We will see you next year. It's good this way, George."

"I just want to see my Little Lawrence again before I have to cut out. I mean, before I get back to work. A boy should know his grandfather. Have some memorable connections to him too, don't you think, Lisa? You mother would want that. Just five minutes? Later on, before I have to leave town?"

Lisa understood the power of his aging magnetism, the leftover bit infused with beggary that had not yet seeped out and poisoned the ground around him.

George returned in the evening wearing a gray sweat suit, his tour bus getup. He brought a gift, a rainbow toy xylophone that had been wrapped in a wrinkled plastic drugstore bag. "Never too early to get them started with the music. He might have the gene."

Lisa thanked George, who proceeded to tap out a happy melody for Lawrence, who in turn responded with spit bubbles and dancing eyes.

"See, my grandson likes it! You had the goods, daughter. I suppose you're no longer playing the violin? Your mother and I thought you might be in a concert hall one day."

The violin had been sold by her mother the day after Lisa's high school graduation, perhaps at the same pawn shop visited the day before.

"No time for that. I haven't touched a musical instrument in years. Lawrence is the priority now. That and the rent, you know."

"That's too bad. You should fill your life with beautiful things, like music. Not just be burdened with responsibilities and troubles." George looked around the room. His demeanor hardened. "But I do see you like my beautiful bracelet." He pointed to a side table, where the bracelet draped a mail bin filled with bills, coupons, and grocery store flyers.

"Believe me. It's tacky. I would never wear such a thing."

"You want it? It's yours. Consider it a gift for the baby. You can tell him the story I told you. It's all about love. He'll appreciate that one day. You'll see."

"I will find other things for him to appreciate about you, George, besides some tale about your secondhand jewelry." Lisa reached for the bracelet. "You may need this one day soon. More than Lawrence will need it later."

"OK. He's got the toy. You'll tell him that his grandpapa gave it to him, won't you? The months are going to go by quickly. He's going to be talking before you know it. You'll let him listen to some of the old records? Tell him that's his granddaddy's bass-playing he's hearing?" George plucked out a riff on his ever-present air bass guitar; he repeated the notes of the line as if he truly wanted Lisa to memorize it and replay it later for Lawrence.

"We'll see you next year, George. You can tell him yourself. Bring your actual instrument. We'll have a little concert. How about that?" Lisa let go of a smile for George then led him out the door and into the dusky evening.

"Have it your way. I always let you have your way most of the time. You have to give me some credit for that, and you turned out okay."

Lisa stretched out her arm as long as she could to hand the bracelet over to George. He opened his shaking hand, but it failed to meet hers. Between them, the bracelet fell to the concrete walkway. Two of the diamonds broke free from their settings and rolled to the edge of Lisa's feet. She squatted to gather the jewels and the bracelet. With an apologetic grimace, she offered the broken bracelet to George. "It's okay. They should pop right back in. Good as new," she said.

"How about you just keep the diamonds," he said as he examined the contents of Lisa's cupped hands. George slipped the bracelet onto his wrist. "See, they came from the *L*. It's meant to be. Somebody is trying to tell us something. Save them for Little Lawrence."

Resigned, Lisa waved him off and watched his car disappear into the night air. Before putting Lawrence to bed, she put the diamonds in a small white envelope, labeling it with an *L* and leaving blank spaces for a *Y* and an *A* that would come much later. Much later.

Collier Road

(1978)

The real-life sound of concrete meeting glass interrupted TV, a *Good Times* wedding episode where sister Thelma marries a football player. Shanice and Yolanda Madison abandoned the summer rerun, and four skinny legs propelled by dusty bare feet raced to the front door, wide open on a much-welcomed and rare breezy August night.

"You a dead nigger!" Mr. Lee was out in the street shouting, while scowling at his grown son, Larry, and hovering near the shattered front windshield of the brown and beige '73 Chevy Nova separating the two. A chain reaction of flicking lights crept down inclined Collier Road and shadowy figures eased into the folds of curtain sheers, but nobody dared go outside and address the commotion.

"Bring it on, old man," Larry said, his voice anchored by soul; a graveyard shift radio D.J. right there on the asphalt. He backtracked from the car and taunted his flabby father by flexing smooth brown mounds of muscle in his biceps and pointing at his thug's gut—a scarred steel paunch, always readied for sucker punches, bullets fired from a .22— whatever it had coming. Mr. Lee opted for another concrete block. Into the center of the driver's side window of the Nova, he delivered a two-handed strike. *Crash!*

He seemed proud of the damage he'd done to an innocent secondhand car, its two-toned body freshly washed and gleaming under gold-tinged street lighting. Mr. Lee flailed his arms about and deliriously repeated, "You a dead nigger, Larry Lee! Dead!"

Larry laughed and calmly fired up a cigarette, even as his only means of transportation was being destroyed before his and the spying neighbors' eyes. This ratcheted Mr. Lee's anger to seething. With open palm chops accentuated by Kung Fu grunts, he forced the remaining stubborn window pieces into the car's interior, hoping perhaps to increase the cost of a cleanup effort unemployed Larry surely didn't have the funds for.

The honey-colored, pumpkin-shaped faces of Shanice and Yolanda winced at the exchange of profanities, threats and low-blow insults. But they kept their eyes fixed on the scene until, from the distant sofa, came their father Joe's stern voice: "Girls! Get from out of that door! And Betty, call the cops. Them Lees is at it again."

The two sisters regrouped on the top bunk in their darkened bedroom; their window at the front of their one-story ranch house provided just as good a view of the street. Meanwhile, in the kitchen, their mother, Betty, could be heard on the phone with the police.

"L-E-E. Lee. L-E-E…" she said, slowly, loudly, and clearly to the police operator as if she were talking to one of her special students.

"All she got to say is 'fight on Collier Road!'" whispered Shanice. "The police would know exactly who it is."

Her younger sister, Yolanda, nodded in agreement. The girls divided a cube of Bubble Yum and returned to the fight, framed and muffled by their bedroom window panes, which made watching the scene a bit like sneaking glimpses of an illicit TV movie with the volume on low.

Then Mrs. Lee busted through the fence gates that enclosed the Lee's front yard. She circled around the Nova, wearing a tattered floral robe and hair rollers, raising hysterical cries for heavenly mercy, perhaps hoping to embarrass her husband and eldest son enough to bring about a cease-fire. Mr. Lee shoved his wife away and, in the process, pulled open the front of her robe, revealing mismatched bra and panties sandwiching a shapeless belly comfortably protruding in all directions.

"Oh. My. God!" Yolanda said. She covered her eyes.

"Oh, stop. You are so childish!" Shanice tried to yank Yolanda's hands aside. She resisted until their tussling turned to play slaps and giddy laughter at Mrs. Lee shamelessly standing in the street, hands on hip, breasts nearing the boiling point and bathrobe wafting behind her like Superman's cape.

Three additional broken car windows later, a police cruiser rolled down Collier Road and Mrs. Lee finally discovered modesty. She closed the top of her robe as a pair of young officers, like seasoned referees, ushered each of the combatants to neutral corners. The fight—for that night, the police said—was over.

Stealing the policemen's final line, Joe yelled to his girls that the show was over for the night and to move along, get back to watching TV. Shanice and Yolanda obeyed, but ignored the remainder of the *Good Times* episode; they knew the familiar outcome of the show's storylines anyway: J.J. fouled things up, and the Evans family was stuck in their taped-before-a-live-studio-audience ghettoland for at least one more season. Instead, they imagined endings for the show being staged next door. Did the police drag Mr. Lee and Larry to jail? Maybe they let them off with another warning and drove away, leaving the possibility of a round two eruption later that night. Were the Lees wondering who called the sheriff on them, and would they retaliate? Did Mrs. Lee go put some clothes on?

The next day, Mr. Lee—shamefaced, head bowed like an old hound dog, wearing a favorite sailor's cap and oversized tortoiseshell sunshades—came ringing the Madisons' front doorbell asking if they would accept an apology for his family's behavior. Joe tried to play ignorant, telling Mr. Lee he had no idea why such a visit was necessary. Betty, however, invited Mr. Lee inside and offered him a cold drink. Sitting in the Madisons' dining room, taking sips of grape-flavored Kool Aid and fiddling with the edges of the plastic table covering, Mr. Lee blamed the fight on the multiple personalities of his son: *No Account Larry* being unemployed, *Shiftless Larry* smoking weed, *Trifling Larry* sneaking around with skanky trailer park white girls and ducking them into his house.

Joe raised an eyebrow and nodded at his girls before Mr. Lee could elaborate. Betty and Mr. Lee agreed that parenting children of any age was hard work, but the Lord rewards the dedicated and the persistent. Eventually, Joe sat quiet, waiting for the last drop of purple Kool Aid to be gone, and Mr. Lee along with it.

"That's it. Next time there's a fight on Collier Road, we're moving," Joe announced as Mr. Lee, barely out of earshot,

plodded down the porch steps outside. The proclamation
arrived like many other important decisions Joe had made.
Facts gave evidence to some tipping point; life called for
quick action. The Madisons had scraped and saved, and with
Joe now securely entrenched as a supervisor at the county's
parks and recreation department, plus Betty's reliable
income from the school system, they were poised to move
out, move up.

"You can't be serious, Joe. I mean, all because of the
Lees?"

"Just think of the girls," Joe said. "Being exposed to that
all the time. It will have an effect on them for sure." Joe
motioned to the front door and the foreboding "that"
festering out on Collier Road. *That.* That mess. That ghetto,
lowlife, ignorant tangled mess of unproductive lives,
irresponsibility, and shameless getting over, as he liked to say,
shaking his head at a most despised mentality. Everything
they escaped from downtown began to emerge on Collier
Road, but in a more aggressive, cancerous form. Guns would
be next, Joe assured. "Just think of the girls."

Joe targeted Betty's soft spot with a familiar discussion-
ender that appealed to her desire to provide the best for her
children. A short dozen years before, Collier Road seemed
just that. Proudly sprouting from golf course-worthy greens
of sculpted hedges and Bermuda grass, a trail of tidy new
homes protected the hopes of two and half dozen nuclear
families that all settled in within a few years of each other,
who all wanted the best for their boys and girls. The
connections ran deep; old schoolmates, ex-boyfriends,
fraternity brothers, in-laws, family friends for generations—
all became neighbors on Collier Road.

As cheap brickwork, bad foundations in hardened red clay, and a series of skillfully executed daytime robberies began sapping optimism, two of the better families—one headed by an M.D., the other by one of the first black engineers hired at the nuclear materials plant—moved away. The Lees slipped into the engineer's house a few months later. No Mayflower moving van or anything comparably civilized, just a caravan of dented pickups stacked to ridiculous heights with plastic orange furniture, saggy stained mattresses, framed prints of fake African queens and rolls of bright red shag carpeting, tangled strings of beads, lamps and piles of clothing, a ragtag assortment of stereo equipment, and more half-naked African queens. Betty did the right thing, carrying over a welcoming lemon cake and taking her girls to meet the new family's kids, who turned out to be three grown men, who didn't seem to have steady work and whose residencies were unclear. Their leering crust-filled eyes, snail-paced speech patterns, and ever-present Newports frightened Shanice and Yolanda. The signals were obvious: The Lee boys—Larry Lee, Smokey Lee, and Gerard Lee—were penitentiary-bound bad boys, like Collier Road had never seen before.

"Hey, y'all," the Lee boys would say to their little neighbors in syrupy mumbles while glued to folding chairs in their driveway, intermittently lifting barbells, getting their Afros picked and plaited, downing cans of A&W, arguing over games of spades, or getting up to work under the hood of the Nova—which, despite a glamorously souped-up exterior, always seemed to be under mechanical repair. Shanice and Yolanda learned to wave back cautiously, and then be on their way. To the park, to school, to church, to piano practice and back inside for afternoon TV.

"They're like prisoners in their own house," Joe said. The girls mocked their inmate status with prison banter they heard on *The Longest Yard*, a movie they'd snuck and saw on Channel 6's Midnight Cinema. "No way to raise children." Joe pounded fist to palm, directing his eyes at the picture window and Mr. Lee, across the street locking the gates of his front yard. He shook his head. The Lees had put up a chain-link fence around their front yard—an egregious violation of unwritten Collier Road homeowners' codes—to keep danger out, when they were the ones endangering the spirits and property values of everyone else.

Sunday, driving home from church with a rousing morning message still buzzing about in their heads, the Madisons went house hunting. New enclaves were spreading out in all directions away from the center of the city. Swaths of bland dirt canvases, considered "the country" just a few years prior, were now painted brilliantly with new spiraling black-tar roadways, sodded green lawns, azaleas, sparkling unsoiled white cement driveways, and brown brick homes with double garages. Joe had stopped for ice cream and, with their tongues lapping Fudgescicles, the Madisons slowed to a parade roll to gawk and gaze at the new homes being built in Chastleton Estates.

"Estates. Sounds prestigious. Maybe a bit pretentious. Out of our league," Betty said. "I don't know, Joe. I just don't know."

"We can afford it, Betty," Joe reassured. The houses were deceptively good-sized, not big, he maintained, noting the hidden side garages made to look like part of the houses' interiors. Another family, also in Sunday dress, drove up to

2816 Chastleton Estates Drive, a "sold" sign leaning against its brick façade. The father of the family, a preacher-looking fellow in a three-piece suit, ordered his teenaged sons to pick up trash left behind by the builders. They dutifully obliged without complaint. The man waved to Joe, and Joe waved back. They both smiled eager reassuring smiles like they were happy to see one another, but were hesitant to start a conversation with forty yards between them. Instead, Joe encouraged everyone to acknowledge their potential new neighbors and wondered aloud about what the man's mortgage payments were going to be.

Even a hundred dollars more a month would be doable, feasible, definitely worth his daughters' futures. Betty and Joe drifted down the road into a fog of finance talk, speculating that it might be time to act as interest rates seemed to be on a permanently rising escalator. Shanice and Yolanda finished their ice creams in silence, which was in abundance in Chastleton Estates. No bass pumping from stereo speakers. No sitcom laugh tracks seeping through cracked windows. No yelling kids or skidding bicycles. No one visiting or laughing on front porches. It was completely noiseless.

During the drive home, Shanice and Yolanda suppressed protestations stirring within, and nodded in response to their father listing the benefits of moving to a place like Chastleton Estates. As Joe, who'd never picked up a tennis racket in his life, was gushing on about the possibility of living yards from the tennis courts the county recreation department planned to build in the center of Chastleton, the Madisons turned the corner onto their Collier Road estate, where Mrs. Lee emerged from their front yard.

"Goodness, what does she want?" Joe put the car in park

and managed a hearty hello above the sound of Betty, Shanice, and Yolanda slamming car doors in unison. With crossed arms clutching herself as if to prevent her body from disintegrating, Mrs. Lee confided that she had gone to church to pray over her husband's and son's conflagration, and per instructions from the Lord, she'd come over to apologize.

Betty gave Mrs. Lee an impromptu hug and repeated the consoling line she'd offered to Mr. Lee, the one about the difficulty of raising children, empathetically adding "in these troubled times," in apparent reference to nothing in particular. Mrs. Lee said that she wanted to make it up to the neighbors in the form of a barbeque to be held in the Lee's front yard.

Betty smiled and a longing musical phrase overtook her voice. "That'll be nice." She volunteered to bring appropriate sides so Mrs. Lee wouldn't have to do all the work. In minutes, the front-yard cookout turned into an all-out block party, a Collier Road social event to rebirth the strained ties between neighbors new and old.

Larry and his brother, Smokey, worked all Friday night to wire their stereo speakers out into their front yard, announcing the success of their patchwork with the rubbery funk of the Bar-Kays at 7:30 the next morning. The third Lee brother, Gerard, stood in the middle of the street and gave the setup an approving fist pump as they tested the volume knob. Around 10:30 a.m., Mr. Lee began manning hand-formed hamburger patties and hacked-up chicken parts over an open flame. He burned the first batch and threw away the blackened thighs. "Why you do that? They still good!" Larry shouted over the music.

Watching from their bedroom window, Shanice and Yolanda held their breath. But Mr. Lee ignored his son, staving off an untimely disruption on such an important day.

Mrs. Lee appeared around noon to watch over card tables filled with foil-covered containers of salads and sides and whoosh away bodacious flies. The Lees froze in a respectable picture-perfect pose and waited for their neighbors to arrive.

"Anybody over there yet?" Joe asked Shanice and Yolanda, who had moved their morning scouting activities to the Madisons' living room picture window.

"Nobody yet. But it's time. Can we go? The food looks good."

"No. Let's not be the first."

Betty held casserole dishes in the open palms of her hand, as if practicing presenting them to Mrs. Lee. "This is silly. We're their neighbors. Let's just go."

"Five minutes," Joe ordered. "Let's give them five minutes."

Standing in their doorway, the Madisons waited and watched. No one showed up, not a car passed, and not a front door from a house on the street opened.

"That's it. This is ridiculous, let's go." Betty ripped open the door, and, before Joe could respond, sang out to the gathered Lees, "Smells delicious!"

Mrs. Lee waved back. A veil of relief seemed to fall over her. She met the Madisons halfway, complimenting Betty on her summer squash casserole before she knew what it was. Joe directed the girls to take seats at one of the card tables.

Slowly, a nervous trickle of neighbors followed the Madisons to the party. The Lee brothers got the music pumping. Charcoal smoke meandered about the confining, fenced-in front yard filled with tense laughter and conversation as all waited for a signal to dive into the food table. Shanice and Yolanda un-perched themselves from the children's table and circulated, catching snippets of neighborly topics: the start of the upcoming school year, complaints about the county's plan to upgrade the drainage system, and the whispered recaps of the Lees latest fight.

"I blame the parents," Mrs. Walden from up the street said to her sister-in-law, Mrs. Maxwell, who also happened to be her next-door neighbor. The two women, sipping golden-brown iced tea from oversized plastic tumblers, had welded their wiry frames to metal folding chairs lodged in a corner of the yard. It was surely a continuation of a dialogue begun earlier, probably on the phone, but maybe over the fence that separated their twin plots. They wagged protruding bottom lips in mutual disgust.

"Grown men have to become responsible at some point in their lives. This generation was given too much." Mrs. Walden put down her tea and pointed towards the Nova parked in the carport, its windows covered with plastic bags and layers of poor-performing masking tape. "They never had to sacrifice like our generation did. Those boys don't even have to pay rent."

Mrs. Maxwell whipped over a look of sheer disdain towards the Lee boys, who were standing in a huddle, swallowing burgers, sucking on barbecued chicken wings, spooning up pork-and-beans and potato salad, bursting into loud laughter every ten seconds, ignoring their unfed neighbors. The three of them must have had seven burgers between them. "Don't even have the manners to serve their guests first."

Betty whispered something to Mrs. Lee and the two of them started unwrapping all the food on the table, including the vegetable salads and casseroles the Lee boys had skipped. She announced that the food table was officially open, and thanked Mrs. Lee for doing all the cooking. Betty led the neighbors in polite applause for Mrs. Lee and then the Lees as a whole. Joe smiled at his wife, who always had a knack for saying and doing the right things, making uncomfortable people feel comforted in all kinds of situations. That kind of graciousness was the trait he hoped most she'd pass on to his girls. Betty motioned to one of the Lee boys to lower the volume of their music. Then she said a prayer, garnering a hearty unclaimed *Amen* after praying for the continuation of neighborly love for all the residents and homeowners on Collier Road and its environs.

"Good God, let's eat," Larry said, concluding the final chorus of Amens that followed Betty's prayer. The Lee boys quickly turned back up the volume on the stereo.

"If there's anything left," Mrs. Walden shouted over the sounds of Mother's Finest.

Betty pointed Yolanda and Shanice to the rear of the forming food line. The Madisons had become the de facto hosts, to show the neighbors their solidarity with the Lees, and to show the Lees how to be neighborly. Joe went along with Betty's conspiring; her silent signals sent him to assist Mr. Lee at the grill.

Yolanda and Shanice fanned their sweaty faces with paper plates and sulked, eyeing the rapid depletion of the once bountiful mound of hamburgers that had been put out.

"They all going to be gone by the time we get up there,"

Yolanda said. "Will you split one with me if you get one first?" she pleaded to her big sister, who was ordained, by birth order, to look out for her little sister.

"Sure."

It proved an un-sisterly hollow answer. When Shanice reached the food table, she commandeered a bun, and slid within it the last freshly-grilled burger. She carefully prepared the toppings: ketchup, lettuce, a three-inch dill pickle spear. Then, with Yolanda watching in horror, Shanice smeared the bun and burger with a knife-full of bright yellow mustard.

"Ugh! You know I hate mustard," Yolanda said.

Shanice twisted her hips and let go of a wry grin. She took a bite into the burger and licked her lips as if performing for a McDonald's commercial. "And I like mustard."

"You want it all? Well, you can have it."

Tears dripped from Yolanda's eyes and, before emitting a piercing wail, she reached for the hamburger, balanced its soggy bun in the palm of her tiny hand, and shoved it towards her sister's smirk—a pie-in-the face response inspired by the previous afternoon's *Brady Bunch* rerun.

In one fluid movement, Shanice wiped her burger grease and condiment-covered cheeks and slapped her sister's forehead. Hard. The Lee boys all doubled over in laughter, cooing and alternately punctuating each returned slap with an exclamation. The tornado of slaps twisted groundward. Betty grimaced and charged towards her girls, conjoined into one and rolling on the grass, mustard spreading from face to face, gluing stray weeds from the Lee's lawn to their foreheads and on their freshly ironed sundresses. Joe followed behind and scooped up his daughters.

"Enough of *that*." Joe turned and nodded feverishly. "You see! You see the influence this neighborhood has on them? You now understand why we have to move?"

Betty, flooded with embarrassment, yanked her girls from beneath the clutches of their father's biceps. The insulted and gaped-mouth residents of Collier Road parted a path.

"Humph," Mrs. Maxwell said, for all to hear. "I blame nobody but the parents." Repeating herself, she defiantly accented each word as Joe and Betty and Shanice and Yolanda made their way through the yard without a backward glance.

The Photograph

(2004)

As if it were an award from some Civil Rights competition, a bust of MLK occupied a prominent spot on the bookshelf. A layer of dust sheeted the plastic exterior of Martin's head—the size of a small coconut—as well as an adjacent row of anonymous hardbacks bound in burgundy or green hues ranging between autumn grass and Army. I'd imagined that the books had been stolen from a library or perhaps ordered from some "of-the-month" catalog years and years ago. The rest of the house reeked of a similar stale history, not quite the color I expected to find in the home of a couple of Southern-fried ex-hippies.

I'd been sent to profile Bracy and Annabelle Lee McClure for a special edition commemorating the 150th anniversary of my newspaper, *A Sesquicentennial of Stories*. I was told the couple gained their notoriety by way of a memorable photograph that appeared in the paper in early March, 1969: Two drugged-out, ill-fed graduate students standing on the steps of the county courthouse in the midst of a protest, seemingly oblivious to a smoldering American flag draping their embrace. For the special edition, they'd be the sole icons representing the activist portion of the 1960s. My editor ticked off some themes to consider in a thousand words, as she hovered over my desk envisioning the final copy. "How did it happen? What were they thinking? Have they now become respectable citizens?"

"Respect?" I whispered, absently scripting the word in the air to settle on a story node, the way a New Age J-school professor taught us to do my freshman year.

"A thousand words," she then reminded. "And make sure we get a picture of these McClures, maybe one duplicating their famed pose. Even in the Internet age, people still like having their picture in the paper." My editor sounded as if she were trying to convince herself of that.

So these McClures, they lived on a street named in honor of a confederate colonel: Farrell Way. Canopied by soaring oaks, a statue of the colonel watched over a well-kept median and weary brick homes lining the street. It would be an old-money neighborhood except all the money had long been transformed into college degrees, red wine, annual trips to Europe, and other dubious investments. Bracy McClure taught history at the state university, so his reliable professor's income kept the lights burning, the water running, and the food bowls filled for an extended family of cats that shared living arrangements with their human benefactors. Annabelle sold watercolor paintings every six months, and supposedly these renderings of Georgia's antebellum mansions, azalea gardens, and sun-soaked Golden Isles waterscapes contributed something to their household income as well. All of this I learned from my editor, who charged me with getting the quirky couple to share their thoughts on the newspaper's famed photograph of the act, which sparked an editorial series on the desecration of the flag and a city ordinance against the specific act of unauthorized burning of any federal symbol on public property. The photographer who took the picture had moved away and was an undistinguished part of the story my editor assured, so no need to track him down. Just get the old hippies to talk about what happened on the courthouse steps and how they'd evolved from town outcasts to whatever they had become—the quirky neighbors who keep quiet and bother no one.

The local desk was in charge of the special edition, farming some work out to the folks in *Sports* and *Life* to piece together 150 years of athletic and social history covered by the paper. Now, supposedly, the McClures hinted they'd only talk to a black reporter about the photograph, perhaps issuing a challenge to test if the paper had any. My byline— Ian O'Neal—gave no clue.

Having hastily disappeared upstairs to find a bathrobe after I arrived, Bracy came back down and produced a handshake. His wiry body sprouted in all directions—bones and angles jutted from his shoulders and knees; long, gnarly toes stretched freely from leather man-sandals, the braided sling-back kind they don't sell anymore. I calculated that he should have been on the backside of middle age, but he looked to be a man twenty years older than that.

"Son," he said, before wincing and flashing a set of teeth slathered with peanut butter. "How are they treating you at *The Journal?*"

"Fine," I said curtly, wanting to show that I was all business. "Is your wife going to join us?"

"Anna will be over in a minute. She's piddling around in

her studio. One never knows when the artistic muse will smack her, so she's been at it all morning." Bracy McClure eased his body into a chair, a worn director's seat in the middle of the living room. A cushiony chair was offered to me. I took it after a quick inspection of the soiled and depressed seat.

"Now, the picture?"

"You mean this one?" Anna appeared in the doorway of a side room—apparently a garage-turned-art studio—with a large canvas in hand. A slight woman with thin reddish hair, she turned the board around and revealed the morning's work. In breezy faint watercolors, she had rendered a copy of the photograph, her painted version of the American flag sporting tropical-flavored pastels. The figures in the painting appeared as dusty apparitions, outlined with thin gray lines. Her courthouse steps vanished into golden sunlight that washed the entire top third of the canvas.

"This woman of mine!" Bracy declared as Anna walked towards us. He reached for the painting and lodged it against his waist to get a better-angled view. "Would be nice to get a photograph of this, yes? You didn't bring a camera, did you?"

I was happy they were willing to be photographed and introduced the idea themselves. Getting a shot with the painting would be a bonus, so I took a few quick snaps of the McClures posing with it. They seemed to be taken back in time by the painting's dreamy expressionism, mesmerized into a moment of silence.

"Now, back to the original photo," I said. "It seems you two are very proud of it."

"You're surprised?" Anna asked.

"Well, are you? Proud of it?"

Anna wagged a finger at me. "It was a defining moment. Didn't change the world, but it challenged minds. Even the microscopic two-brain-celled minds littered about this town." Her tone lowered. "Like good art is supposed to do."

"So, you think this news photo was art?" I handed the two of them photocopies of the picture. They took studied looks. Anna then reached for and raised a cup of tea that had been surreptitiously steeping on a coffee table cluttered with magazines and thick old art books. She brought the cup close to her face and blew gently against faint steam. "Sometimes, art isn't art until someone declares it so. I declared it so because the photograph changed the discussion. Do you know what the protest was all about, Mr.—?"

"O'Neal."

"Well, Mr. O'Neal, a young African-American man was beaten by the cops. Dragged from his motorcycle and clubbed silly for no good reason at all. They said he'd stolen a pocketbook from a coed or some such nonsense, and then he resisted arrest after challenging the accusation. People who looked like me and Bracy made all kinds of justifications, but no one wanted to face the truth."

Bracy gazed lovingly at his wife; her controlled seething prompted an odd, admiring smile on his face.

I dropped my notepad in my lap and held my palms out as if to balance the two events on a scale. "So, this kid was beaten and, in protest, you two draped yourselves in a flag that had been set on fire?"

"Yes, if you want to put it in the fashion of cause and effect, those are the sequence of the facts of the events. It didn't heal his wounds, but the establishment was challenged on its actions and a statement was made."

"And things quieted down in this town after that," Bracy added. "People saw white people like themselves taking a stand for something they knew to be wrong. It affected hearts. A few. We didn't have some of the problems other Southern cities had. I'd like to believe we had something to do with that."

"So then, take me back to that day," I said. "Like, who struck the first match? Where did the flag come from? Did you two just go out and buy it from the K-Mart? How much did it cost?"

Bracy laughed. "Good one. Let's see, where did that piece of cloth come from? We surely must have stolen it from somewhere. Off the flagpole at one of the high schools, maybe?"

"Who knows," Anna answered. "A school, a post office, who knows. Why write about such trivialities, Mr. O'Neal, considering the seriousness of the times and the issue? What about the boy who was beaten? The policemen who weren't punished? Your paper's editorials in the aftermath defending 'law and order'? Why don't you write about that?"

"Ma'am, it's about the photograph, that's all. Notable and memorable pictures that have been in the paper over the decades."

She rose, tightened the belt around her faded napped robe, and turned her back to me. "Well then, I want no part of this."

Bracy winked, and then whispered to me, "I'll take care of her. Wait here." He followed Anna back out into her garage studio and shut the door behind him. I heard their muffled voices and then nothing. Then their voices again and the movement of objects. As this continued, I pulled out the digital camera and snapped four more shots of Anna's painting leaning against the coffee table. Bracy returned with a big smile.

"Mr. O'Neal, how about we continue this discussion tomorrow? Anna's just having a bad day. They come, but they go. Tomorrow should be good."

I agreed to meet the McClures again, at a diner across the street from the courthouse where the photograph was taken, two short blocks from our news building. The diner was busy and loud—lawyers yakking away on cellular phones, servers handling dishware, a diverse group wearing juror's badges making small talk beneath a TV showing a cable news program. I asked short, pointed questions atop the noise. The McClures gave short answers until I asked them if they would walk across the street to the courthouse and show me exactly where the picture was taken. Anna shook her head. She didn't want to recreate the scene. She hated such sentiments, she said, recalling the pathetic congratulatory anniversary marches that had sprung up in the eighties.

"Nostalgic fluff. What does it accomplish? What message does it send? Your generation should do its own thing. You may only get one chance to make a difference. Don't miss yours celebrating someone else's past glory."

I prodded on. "So, about the tenth step up, you and Bracy stopped there, right? Did you just walk up there with the flag? Did the other protesters notice? What were they doing? How long was it before somebody noticed? Did you see the photographer? Did the photographer say anything to you all?"

"It was a protest, son," Bracy said. "A few dozen or so from the university decided we had to do something. We'd met for lunch right at this very spot. The setup was different then and the place had a different name, but I believe we were actually in a booth over there."

Bracy pointed to the jurors: three black women, two white men, and three white women crowded into a pair of booths. They laughed together like old friends, but everyone in the place could hear the conversation was idle chat—commentary on the choice of TV channels, the saltiness of the diner food, the annoying but necessary particulars of post-9/11 courtroom security.

Bracy continued. "We all argued about what exactly we should do: protest in shifts, storm the courthouse door all at once, or something dramatic. We never did come to any consensus, except that everybody decided they would just do whatever felt right." Bracy laughed and gave me a fatherly shoulder grab. "That's how we did things in those days son. No planning or real goal setting. If it felt good, we did it."

"But the end result had an impact," Anna said. "And that's *all* this little piece of yours needs to be focusing on."

Bracy McClure agreed to head over to the courthouse steps after lunch, but Anna refused. She was determined to have no parts of it. I had called over a photographer from the paper to meet us, and maybe get at least one shot of Bracy on the steps.

"Right about there?" I asked Bracy as he wiped mayonnaise from the creases of his mouth.

"I'd say so. You seem to be making a lot of fuss over all this, Mr. O'Neal. Surely there must be hundreds of other photos you all will be using in your special edition worth more attention. Pictures of mayors or governors or presidents who visited? Some sports or movie celebrities who passed through town?"

I blamed the editor for my necessary persistence, and then tried to get some sympathy. "They just really want a good picture about the picture. Nobody's going to read the words. Your wife shouldn't be too worried. It's not that deep."

The photographer tapped his watch. "You ready, mister?"

I pulled a small American flag from my notebook that I had bought that morning from a drugstore. "How about just a quick shot on the historic spot, exactly where the original photo was taken?"

Bracy hesitated, wiped away crumbs from his pants then heaved his body into an erect stance. "OK, Mr. O'Neal." He reached for the flag without me asking him to pose with it. He held the stem of the flag between the fingers of his cupped hands. The photographer took five or six quick shots.

"Thanks. We're done," the photographer said. He quickly began packing his equipment.

"That's it?" Bracy asked.

"Looks like it."

I shook Bracy's hand and walked away, making my way over to a high school for another assignment: An interview with a retired high school football coach to discuss a 1972 photo of him striking a Heisman pose with a pair of his running backs, one of whom would go on to star for the university.

The next day, I got an email from a photo editor at the paper. "Notice anything strange?" he asked in the subject line. He'd laid out the photograph of the McClures taken in the sixties alongside the one of Bracy taken just the day before. He attached the combined digital image to the email.

Bracy's stance in the newer photo was a little strained and crooked, but he had aged. Nothing strange about that. I looked closer at the old photo. Bracy and Anna's bodies cast a long abstract shadow that angled down steep steps. Their joint bodies standing straight and the shadow seemed to form a sundial, the late afternoon sun apparently beating down from the left side of the picture.

With a copy of his email in my hand, I went down to see George, the photo editor who'd sent the email. A tattooed and pierced twentysomething, he nonchalantly answered my puzzled look before I said anything.

"You don't see it, do you?"

"See what?" I asked.

"The steps, the shadows, man. They're different. No way these pictures were taken on the same set of steps. The old picture, those steps—that's not the county courthouse."

With the cropped and zoomed-in visual evidence on his computer monitor, he explained what he'd uncovered from his photo-detective work: There was a difference in the steepness of the two sets of steps, a difference in the positioning of the shadow of what should have been produced by the same afternoon-sun angle, and a difference in the depth of the vanishing point—much further back in the older photograph than it was in the new one. "White marble steps in both pictures to be sure, but two different buildings." George pointed at the blowup of the old picture. "Unless they've done some major renovations and changed the way the sun shines, that's not the courthouse down the block. There's your story, brother. That older photo wasn't taken at the courthouse. Something is fishy here."

I took another look at the old photo. The sun seemed to be shining overhead. Like the ghostly images in Anna's painting, the couple seemed to be two-dimensional figures plastered into the scene where they didn't quite belong. "Can't be too many buildings in town with such grand marble steps," George said. "Maybe it was taken in front of a building on campus at the university? If I were a betting man, I'd put money on it that the old photo was staged, or at least taken at some other event, not the protest at the courthouse. With a little reporter's gumshoe work, I think you can find where these folks really took that picture."

I thanked George and headed to that evening's assignment, a protest against the university for wanting to demolish a housing project to make way for a new student union. While there, I could take a walk around, maybe see if I could find the mystery steps.

I interviewed only one protestor, drawn to her by the lengthy hand-written sign she held up: "Yes to housing for the poor, No to a playground for rich kids." She, one of the few whites in the crowd, introduced herself as a sociology grad student at the university. She pleaded the case for her cause with fretful intensity. "No need for the state to be subsidizing such an anachronistic building," she told me over the monotonous chants of her fellow protestors. "The student center we have now is perfectly fine and underutilized. These kids already have their 'third places,' their coffee shops, the library lounge, their bars and fancy apartment clubhouses. Why should the state displace poor people, once again, to create just another hangout where these kids will do nothing but glaze over laptop computer screens?"

I nodded, and to let the woman know I'd gotten the gist of her thesis, closed my notepad. As their hoarse voices trailed off, the dusk light settled over the protesters and everything ended abruptly without incident or any response from the university officials, who probably had long escaped the administration building. Those who were residents of the housing project headed back to their homes across the street, knowing full well the bulldozers would soon be maneuvering into place. So much for a student protest having any impact. In the evening light, I then strolled around campus to look for any building with marble steps. There were, indeed, a few. The steps in front of the literary society building were particularly grand. The building, bearing a name borrowed from ancient Greece, looked to not get much use and was shrouded by a massive modern library being constructed for the law school. I took a few photos of the steps and left.

Heading home, I drove along Farrell Way, slowing down in front of the McClures' house. Fiery lights, as if from a flame, flickered in small window panes lining the garage door. I got curious. One of the McClures' cats, standing guard under the lights of the front porch, spotted me as I parked in front of the house and walked towards the garage.

I peeked inside the windows and saw Bracy embracing Anna from behind while her arms angrily flailed above a small fire burning in a metal bucket. He managed to push her aside and extinguish the flame, and then opened a side door to wave away the fumes. Anna drew a fist at the back wall where dozens of small paintings hung in random spots. My gaze panned backwards and I slowly began to see the paintings, many of them variations of the scene of their famous photograph, journeying through a history of artistic styles.

Bracy reached for a charred rolled-up canvas out of the bucket. He unfurled the painting, the one Anna had completed the morning of my visit, realizing that too much had been burnt to save it. He folded it into fours. The cat rustled from the porch, around to the garage, and scratched at the garage door. I stepped away as Bracy, startled, turned and saw me there. I saw tears in his eyes. We said nothing to each other. I backed away from the garage windows and retreated to my car. Later that evening, on my laptop, I crafted the beginning of my story about the photograph:

On a cool spring morning in 1969, two university graduate students protesting the arrest of a young black man stood on the County Courthouse steps and inadvertently created art.

Cotton Compress

They marched into the yard like survivors of a massive blizzard. Cotton dust powdered the tops of their denim caps and unkempt heads, despite Vina's repeated directive to "Brush it off, leave it outside!" Their conversations, bounded by boisterous, doubled-over laughs, carried on all the way to the porch and into the orderly line they formed at the kitchen door. They cussed the most incompetent foreman on the planet, teased one fellow about his wife's tarbaby complexion, and longed for the day when 'Miss Vina' would forget her ornery widow ways. Then, getting a whiff of the kitchen aromas, they speculated on the source: *Rabbit? Squirrel?* Vina would never tell, assuring them as long as it adequately sustained them until quitting time, what difference did it matter what meat made its way into her stew?

Before allowing the men to come inside, Vina carefully raised the morning's concoction upwards to Randolph, her nephew, home for the summer after completing a first year of graduate school up North. "How that taste?"

Randolph answered with a tight-lipped wince. He dashed to the sink, spat, and then positioned his mouth beneath a stream of rust-flavored tap water flowing from the faucet, relieving the peppery burn festering on his tongue. Vina tossed a rag over her hunched shoulder, not bothering to explain what Randolph knew: she used bad meat. Damned near rotten. The pepper masks the stink. The men from the cotton compress wouldn't have it any other way, she'd once said.

Randolph shook his head. "Now this exemplifies the twisted psychosis of the oppressed Negro. Our perceptions of ourselves remain so perversely distorted, we heartedly believe in our inherent inferiority. We can only conceive ourselves as deserving *less than* what we truly deserve. So we eat stinking, rotting meat because the bigoted universe ordains it to be."

"Nephew, if all those words mean 'them lint-headed niggers eat it because they like it,' then yes, I shall find agreement with you. Now, I thank you for coming to visit your old auntie, but erase all that lecturing from the chalkboard inside your brain and help me serve up these bowls before you up and take off. Those empty bellies outside want to be filled with food, not all your college words."

A unique enterprise had been fashioned under the grand shed and in the old warehouses on the other side of Mill Street, directly across the way from Vina's and a row of other tidy clapboard homes. Fortunately so, most would claim, as it provided employment for dozens of its Turpin Hill neighbors. Hour after hour, day after day—save the day of the Lord—bales of cotton paraded into the back of the building and magically transformed into smaller bales for compact and efficient loading onto waiting boxcars destined for mills, ports, and manufacturers in various points North and South. Cotton compressing was *all* they did across the street.

The economics and presumed profitability fascinated Randolph. How long does it take to train a man to operate the powerful machines that squeeze the cotton as tightly as earthly physics allows? How much time and money do the bosses and owners lose to the idiosyncratic ways of their workers' ilk, fickleness, or prevalence for sickness and lies? How does one account for losing productivity to actual aches and pains lodged deeply into their backs and legs? How many fuel-draining railroad trips are subsequently saved by having those noisy machines squeeze six oversized cubes of cotton into the space of one? What deals secured the land beside the railroad tracks? What clandestine negotiations determined the allowable regulated density of the compressed bales? Engineers, accountants, mathematicians, politicians, financiers—a hundred smart men must have reasoned through a hundred ideas to produce the logistics that created the employment that paid the wages that produced the nickels traded daily for Aunt Vina's forsaken stew. The budding socialists back at the university had no appreciation for cooperative invisible hands steering the wheel of innovation, steadied and encouraged by the rewards of free markets.

No time to ponder such thoughts—the noon whistle had blown. Time to ladle stew, five pennies a serving.

The men took their steaming bowls and sat on paint cans lining the walls of Vina's great room, their midday stench rising in the stuffy hot air. Through an open window, periodic breezes brought in the fragrance of dogwoods.

Pleased with her productivity after the last man was served, Vina led Randolph into the center of the congregants, introduced him as her "nephew Randy" and asked for quiet as the lunchtime devotional was about to begin.

Randolph balked. "I'm no preacher, Auntie."

"But your daddy is," one of the men reminded. The youngest in the group had spoken up, defying Aunt Vina's raised hand. "Randy, it's me! Emerson Greene? You remember? We schooled together down at Washington. I made it through the 6th grade. How far did you get?"

Randolph had sailed through college, learned of great European philosophers from sympathetic Jewish professors finding post-war refuge at the Negro schools of Nashville, secured a bachelor's degree in the sociological sciences, and won a fellowship for more in-depth study at the graduate level at a fine university in New York, the grandest city on Earth.

"High school, a little college thereafter," Randolph admitted.

Emerson beamed. "Always knew you'd be destined for great things. Say something erudite! Remember that? Mrs. Williston in 5th grade always wanted her class to be 'erudite.'"

"Eat your stew, Greene," Vina said. "All that fat mouthing and you won't be finished before it's time to get back and you'll lose the one paying job you'll ever have in life." Forgoing the oversized family Bible resting atop the breakfront, Vina retrieved a smaller one reserved for actual reading from the top drawer and blindly flipped to a passage. She swiftly paged through the New Testament and fingered a verse somewhere in the middle. "Now read, Randolph. Read that."

Randolph cleared his throat and obliged, eloquently maneuvering over the textual hurdles placed by King James's

English. He could have pursued the ministry—had he wanted to, had it been demanded of him. As he read, Randolph imagined where he would be if had taken that path, ignoring the message of forgiveness, faith, and devotion his voice read in a good Presbyterian monotone. Vina, however, paid attention. She moaned in agreement after each period and scolded the congregants when Randolph paused between particular pertinent passages. "She should pay *us* for the pleasure of having us listen to her sermons," one of the men whispered to Randolph at the conclusion of the reading.

Randolph relayed this bit of confidence and the rest of the day's encounter to his father later that evening. The senior Randolph, the Reverend, had interrupted his pre-supper reading itinerary: cowboy comics, the newspaper's colored social page, and an inventory of Bible lessons.

"So, what did you learn today?" the Reverend asked. This opening line greeted Randolph often during his formative years, primarily as a reminder to never squander the opportunity to expand the mind, secondarily to consider that the most profound lessons sometimes took a parable form.

"Why has Aunt Vina always used bad meat to make her stew for the men from the cotton warehouses?" Randolph asked. "It's barely palatable, yet they clean their bowls without complaint."

"Is there an insight you're overlooking? What of your aunt's resourcefulness and ingenuity?"

"I doubt that's it," Randolph answered.

"Well, where would the men go if your Aunt Vina were not there? And she'd of course have to charge more for the stew if she purchased and maintained more choice cuts of meat. And the men, don't you think, after four hours straight of bone-tendering real labor, they're hardly seeking culinary delicacies. And what of the sense of purpose Vina now has in her life since the Doctor passed? Perhaps your mother and I should have sent you off to commerce school instead of this one bulging your head with lots of questions instead of answers."

Answers. That was what the cotton compress men needed. Before bed, Randolph grazed the book spines lining the shelf in his room. They represented a year's worth of learning, or at least reading of words. After unpacking them from his trunk, he had shelved them first by course, then by author, and lastly, out of boredom and for aesthetics, by width. Kant, Hegel, Weber, Nietzsche—the names, titles, and schools of thought blur, but the books appeared orderly. Randolph reached for Durkheim's *The Division of Labour in Society,* and then his reading eyeglasses. He read himself to sleep.

Randolph returned to Vina's the next morning, where a bountiful breakfast thankfully cleansed the memory of the taste of the previous day's stew. She could really cook when she wanted to. Randolph silently prayed over the steaming biscuits, ham, stewed tomatoes, eggs, buttered grits, peach slices, and black coffee. "I thank you, Aunt Vina, for cooking and everything else you've done. Your contributions have been a great help in reducing the financial burden."

"Well, you can rest up this summer. Not like those college boys taking to the tobacco fields to earn a little extra cash. I'm sure your father will appreciate your assistance around the church as well." She went about the fuss of her kitchen work. Money never seemed a worry for Vina. The Doctor had left her with a healthy trust administered by some shy mulatto man from Atlanta who'd come down each month in that secondhand Packard of his with checks and legal papers in tow. The checks would stack up over time and Vina signed some directly over to Randolph, the memos indicating the funds should be used for books, tuition balances, or train tickets. Or for treating a coed, one suitable for marriage.

"I am lucky, Aunt Vina, to have means and resources. And it has afforded me the opportunity to now see things and go places, which makes me want things and to see more places. These men at the cotton compress, what have they seen? Where have they been? Most of them probably have not been much further than Turpin Hill for most of their lives."

"What does that matter? They are fortunate to be able to provide for their families what they can. Seeing things and going places would only instill resentment, and constantly remind them of what they cannot ever obtain. No, Randolph, sometimes it's best not to open doors for those never prepared to pass through them. The visions on the other side may only serve to confuse and frustrate."

"You sound like the white man, Auntie. Are they satisfied? Do you honestly believe the men get any sense of accomplishment from the success of their employer's company? Do they feel a part of anything? Has anyone *asked* them?"

"You're not coming in here talking that communism. Is that where the Doctor's money is going? Up there so you can get your head filled with communism?"

"No, no, Aunt Vina. I admire the businessmen over there at the cotton compress. Look what those men have done; it's a fine example of industrial ingenuity rarely celebrated in the Southern states," Randolph said, though he had no idea who *those* men were. Sure, he'd read names in the papers and had seen a few impressive automobiles parked out front, but he didn't know *those* men. But the opportunity presented itself to get to know the men who knew those men; the ones who moved their bales and operated their machines and sweated until they smelled like hogs.

"I have an idea. Instead of the Bible today, I'd like to maybe have a chance to have a discussion with the men." Randolph held up his satchel. "Discuss some of the ideas in my books?"

"You're trying to turn my parlor into a classroom? I'd like to see how that goes over."

"So, can I?"

"As long as one of the contributing authors of one of your books is Christ our Lord, then yes."

"Well, as long as you let me pick out the Bible verse."

"I'm happy to oblige," Vina said.

She cleared her nephew's plate and prepared to heat up her stew pot, which had not been washed clean from the day before—dried gravy remnants lined its rim. Vina nevertheless fired up the burner and tossed in a scoop of rendered lard. As smoke sailed around the kitchen, Randolph retreated to the quiet and clear air of his uncle's old office, a spare adjoining room mostly locked off since his death. In there, Vina had not moved a paper, discarded a patient's file, nor touched the stethoscope dangling from a coat rack. Like a rank of soldiers dutifully awaiting orders, empty pharmaceutical bottles stood in perfect rows in a glass-encased shelf. The Doctor's thick anatomy books had been bound in twine, ready to be discarded or gifted to another physician, but remained undisturbed on his broad mahogany desk. Randolph moved them aside and made space to prepare a lesson for his new class of students.

The stew simmered on and Vina made cornbread. She announced loudly to Randolph that she would offer it at no extra cost. The previous day's conversation perhaps made her feel guilty, Randolph thought. A small victory had been won. Soon after the noon whistle blew, the men filed in with great anticipation. The buttery aroma had seeped across the street.

"What's gotten into you, Miss Vina?" one of them asked, leading the line, hat in hand.

"Don't get used to it," Vina told him. "Just had a bit of extra corn meal to get rid of is all. Too hot to be using my oven anyway. You know my rules: the oven stays off when the thermometer hits eighty. But next week, if I decide to make it, it'll cost you a few cents extra. Nothing comes free in this life."

"Where's that nephew of yours today, Miss Vina?" Randolph heard another ask.

"Oh, he's in there. Wants to conduct a little school for you all." Randolph could hear the chuckles. "Let him know exactly what you all think of that idea."

The men shuffled as one into the parlor and took familiar seats on the paint cans. Emerson Greene greeted Randolph again and provided another recollection of their schooldays—the sporting games they played on crisp fall afternoons and how he'd bested Randolph in base running, hitting, and fielding.

One of the older men interrupted the reminiscing. "What you got on your mind, son? You come here to talk labor?"

"No, no, sir, nothing like that. Just thought maybe instead of the Bible—I mean, instead of *just* the Bible—I could share some of what I have been learning." Randolph pulled three books out of his satchel and held them up as if they were the trinity of knowledge, not just the leftover text from last year's coursework.

"What exactly are you learning to do, Randolph?" Emerson asked.

A quiet disinterest filled the room as the men sopped their stew with the special cornbread and Randolph thought about the question. One learns in order *to do*, not *to think* or *to become* or to grow or even to persuade others to do. You learn to *do* something.

"I am learning how to apply knowledge to solve the problems of our society. Take, for instance, the problem of race. What can we learn about the nature of the human condition so we can in turn understand how the races can better relate to one another?"

"And how will you *do* that?"

"By learning to teach others what I've learned, Emerson. I guess I am learning how to be a teacher."

"And you had to go all the way to New York City to learn that?" someone asked. Snickers scattered about the room. Randolph realized that his elocution and probably even his schoolboy gait, horned-rimmed eyeglasses, and pressed clothes were being mocked. He decided against the book lesson—at least for the day—and posed a question to the men.

"What did you want to do when we were in school? What did you think about becoming in life? Cotton compress men? Emerson, you yourself were just minutes ago bragging of your exploits on the baseball diamond—how you beat me and every boy down at Washington. Did it ever occur to you to evolve those athletic skills into a vocation? A business of your own? And what about the rest of you? When did it become satisfactory for you to be filling your insides with cotton dust, day after day, so some white overseer's overseer could be rewarded with the fruits?" In response, spoons scraped against the sides of bowls. Randolph reached for the Bible Vina set out for him, opened to *Deuteronomy 28*, which turned out to be another Christian plea for obedience and for men to find happiness in their predestinations.

As their inner clocks prompted the men to finish up and stack the bowls on a table beside a doorway—just as Vina had instructed them to do—Emerson grabbed for Randolph's arm. "I'm interested in what you got to say, Randy," he consoled. "Maybe we can meet up after quitting time one evening. Just me and you."

Randolph tried to find an appreciative beam within him, but only mustered a nod.

Vina shut the door behind the last of the men and wiped her hands brusquely on the soiled apron around her waist. Randolph collected all the bowls.

"See, what I told you," she said. "Some of them might be young men, but their kind become old dogs early in life. They don't learn new tricks. I'm sure eager to know how your learning can be applied to them."

—

The Reverend brought out lemonade to Emerson and Randolph as the two sat in opposing swinging chairs on the front porch of his home. A pint of whisky bulged in the side pocket of Emerson's work pants. Randolph had already warned Emerson not to reach for it, no matter how badly he wanted a swig of that instead of the Reverend's always too-syrupy and too-warm lemon water.

"I thank you, Reverend, but you didn't have to trouble yourself," Emerson said.

"Nonsense, son. You've had a long day of honest work. It's my pleasure to serve *you.*"

Emerson laughed after the Reverend went back into the house. "Never a day in my life would my daddy be fetching another grown *colored* man a drink. Not even a white one, the more I think on it. You and yours have always been a different kind of people, Randy."

"How so?" Randolph asked.

"You know. Different."

Randolph did know. His parents owned their property outright, kept lively mums in their yard, and owned bookshelves filled with actual books. His father prayed eloquent prayers of thanks for patience and wisdom, never for wants or resolution. His mother had not held a paying job since she married. No need to agitate Emerson with any defensiveness about all of that. Instead, Randolph asked, "Why did you quit your schooling, Emerson?"

"Quit? It wasn't exactly like it came to me on one particular day that I'd up and stopped going. The words and letters and numbers just got all twisted up in my head and before you know it, I started missing a few days here and there, and then a few more. A year or two later, Daddy had me at the compress tailing him, learning the machines, shining up on the boss man, and I been there ever sense."

"But what's next for you in life?"

"Next is being on time at the compress tomorrow. And on time the day after that. I got a baby girl now." Emerson laughed. "I don't think she stopped eating since she came out of her mama."

"Maybe I could help you with that. You know, help you figure out where you should be going next. That's why you came here, isn't it?"

"Not really, Randy. I just thought you could help me untwist them letters and words. Not trying to solve the world's problems, like you."

"You mean you want me to teach you to read?"

"I can read. I know my letters. I even know a bunch of small words. But maybe you can help me wrestle with them big words, you know, like 'erudite.' I can hear it, say it, and pretty much know what it mean when it come out a person's mouth, but couldn't print all the letters on a piece of paper even if a madman had a pistol to my head."

Dusk had arrived. Randolph took the final sip of his lemonade. Emerson had finished his as well. His palm caressed the pint in his pocket. Randolph motioned that it was finally okay to take that swig, even on a preacher's front porch. Emerson did just that and his gaze turned to the cotton compress roof in the distance.

"Those big words? I can help you with that," Randolph said. Fairly certain he no longer had Emerson's full attention, he gladly repeated the words to himself: I can help him, with *that*.

Glass House

(1998)

Cheryl paused her sweeping, hugged the broom's handle, and rolled her eyes skyward. Who thought it a good idea to put a glass-covered center atrium inside a home, turning it into a greenhouse for human inhabitants? The place had been built in the seventies, during the midst of a national energy crisis. Every owner since the original must have conjured a similar thought, probably immediately after receiving that first summertime utility bill from Georgia Power. At the final walkthrough with Cheryl and Todd, the real estate agent praised the wonders of evening sunlight, shining unfiltered indoors. "You all will be bathing in nature," she marveled and promised. After all those years of suffering through the drabbest of on-base military housing from Belgium to Korea, Todd was completely taken by the prospect of all-day natural lighting. And with no down payment required to rent-to-own the property, the deal couldn't be beat. The agent, however, neglected to mention the dome's leaky seals and the splotchy bird crap mosaics that would develop over time and prompt Sunday afternoon Rorschach tests. And then there were the neighborhood kids inspired to snarky architectural criticism—"Mrs. Thompson, did you know your house looks just like the Starship Enterprise?"

Todd promised Cheryl a practical replacement within a few years after their move-in date. Those few years passed and raindrops began to drip through. He promised to have the leak covered with plywood as a short-term measure. That never happened. Five years hence, standing in the haze of yet another relentless sunbeam, Cheryl knew she had to issue the annual reminder. Something needed to be done about the stupid glass dome.

She put on sunglasses—a routine silent but dramatic protest—and went about the business of corralling her sweepings into the foyer and onto the hardwood of the living room that never had much foot traffic. *No kids. No pets. Rarely a visitor. How does the floor get so dirty?* Failing to arrive at a plausible answer, Cheryl saved her pile in a corner. She'd vacuum it up later.

Next, she set out to wash the series of sliding picture windows spanning the entire front of the house, a more practical manifestation of the builder's vision of 1970s contemporary style. The trees in the yard provided shade in the summer and this glass, thankfully, could be washed without scaffolding or other special industrial equipment. When the pines stretched outward, the oak tree returned to green, and the azaleas bloomed, nature spilled inside like oozing liquid as if the window panes were not even there. Winter was wasted on the South though; fifty degree average temperatures, days colored with lifeless browns, and the ground dusted once a year with the sorriest of sleets or the faintest of snows. Nothing like the cozy white winters of her native Michigan.

Cheryl readied her Windex bottle and squeegee then turned towards the window as if to duel. Just as she pulled the trigger on the bottle and let loose a broad spray of cleaner, she wailed a high-pitched scream. There, on the opposite side of the glass, a man raised up from his crouching stance and waved his hands apologetically. He inched backwards on the front porch, each baby step injecting a tremble up into his body.

"I'm sorry, ma'am. I didn't mean to scare you!" The glass muffled the sound of his nervous voice.

Cheryl traded the Windex bottle for the broom, shouldering it like a rifle. "Who are you? What do you want?"

He was a short and well-dressed man, sporting a blue blazer on this sunny late Saturday morning. Perhaps he was just another nosy neighbor Cheryl had not yet met.

"Didn't mean to startle you. I saw you through the window from the street and thought you couldn't see out." The man tugged the corner of imaginary eyeglass frames on his face. "So I came up for a closer look."

Cheryl felt relieved and removed her sunglasses but kept a firm gaze on the man. She tilted her head and asked again: "What do you want?"

"My name is McRae, ma'am. I used to live here. In this house." The man aimed both of his pointing fingers at his shoes, claiming the property below as his own. "But that was long ago. I'm just passing through and wanted to get a look at the old place. I'm visiting from out of town so I don't get the opportunity often. It brings back such special memories I just had to come by, reminisce a bit. I'll leave you be. I see you have your Saturday cleaning to do. Please accept my apologies."

The man turned and headed to a compact car parked at the curb. Getting a fuller picture of his short stature and gimpy walk, Cheryl again saw no need for alarm, to interrupt Todd's golf game, solicit a neighbor's help or bother the police. She went outside and called to the man as he repeatedly aimed a remote entry key at the stubbornly locked car. "Sir, you said you lived here? In this house?"

He stood silent. She motioned for him to meet her in neutral territory in the middle of the street. She dipped her head and cupped an ear, like an old lady eager for her grandkid's charmed replies. The man ignored the gesture and instead strolled right into the yard, traipsing through cut grass clippings that Todd needed to rake and discard. The man began his own self-guided tour of the property, ticking off memories about long-gone six-foot hedges, the bright orange color the shutters had once been, a swing hung from the oak's sturdiest branch, a grand black wrought iron fence that once gated the carport and the entrance once guarded by twin gold-painted lion statues. "This house was my dad's dream. It only lasted until around the mid-eighties though." The man laughed. "The family's been cursed ever since. Blamed it on this place. But I loved it as a boy." He motioned to the neighboring houses in view, mostly brick split-levels wearing their ages reasonably well. "There are some nice houses out here, but we had the coolest one on the block. When did your family move in, ma'am?"

"It's just me and my husband. We're going into our eighth year," Cheryl said. "Would you like to come inside, Mr. McRae? See what the house looks like now?" If something bad were to happen, well, at least Todd would be home soon.

"Daddy, some might say, was a gangster," the man

revealed between sips of iced tea while sitting at the kitchen table and staring at the new fixtures and countertops Cheryl had installed. The floors remained to be done though. McRae surely noted the incongruence of gray granite, retro-modern appliances and aged dirty-yellow linoleum, clashing like cheap and gaudy silver and gold jewelry. *The floors: another household project Todd scheduled for after his retirement.*

"Is that so?" Cheryl vigorously stirred the remainder of the tea in a pitcher. She poured herself half a glass and took a long, refreshing swig.

"Don't get me wrong. I don't mean Tommy guns or mafia crime family gangster. And not your modern-day street thugs and killers. I mean just your basic run-of-the-mill petty hoodlum stuff, doing the kinds of things people had to do to keep food on the table for their families."

Cheryl inventoried all four thousand square feet of the house, the four toilets, the screened porch with the rarely-lit brick barbeque, the three-car garage and the ten separate rooms, only four of which she and Todd actively used. "So from the proceeds of his lifestyle and with the intent of just trying to feed his family, your father found time and was able to build all of this?"

"Pretty much." McRae cleared out a space on the kitchen table, moving aside a stack of mail awaiting Todd's attention. "It's the invisible hand of the ghetto economy, see. A young project girl with overdue rent steals some New York strips from the Piggly-Wiggly," he said, pin-pointing a location on the tabletop where his economic cycle began. "My daddy buys them at fifty cent on the dollar and has the girl take them to a freezer in the basement of an old country church whose collection plates are running on empty. He turns around and sells them at a ten percent mark-up to the congregants with no appetite for risk and outright stealing but one for nice U.S.D.A.-approved beef. The church gets a fair cut for their storage services and customer base, and Daddy never sets eyes on the goods but makes a nice little profit for coordinating the players and the logistics. Now, multiply that by five or six locations across the city and a couple hundred transactions at each site every month. It's win-win-win for a whole lot of people."

"Well, except the owner of the grocery store and the poor ones who managed to get themselves caught. I'm from Detroit, Mr. McRae. I understand how these things work. But how does one get started in building such a shoplifting conglomerate?"

"I don't think it was exactly a career choice. He had that hustle engrained in him. He started as an errand boy for my granddaddy."

"So your granddaddy was a gangster, too?"

"I'm not making a very good impression, am I? But yes. Does the name Hinton McRae mean anything to you?"

"No, can't say that it does."

McRae nodded. "Oh, yeah, you're not from around here. Still new."

Seven years and Cheryl was still *new*. A military transient in the eyes of the locals. She didn't drop any kids off at an elementary school along with her neighbors, had no local church home with a stained glass window dedicated to a grandma, never shopped in the old downtown department stores, took no sides in the high school football rivalries, and had no family stories about the night of the big race riot in '71 to trade and pass down. She and Todd were permanently newcomers. And here was this McRae, gone long enough to develop a marble-mouth New Yorker's accent and yet comfortable enough to come around stalking the current residents of his childhood home.

"Of course I'm not condoning any of that," said McRae. "And it took a great toll on my family. My daddy did a stint in the prison in Reidsville and after he died, the family ended up owing the whole world more than he ever took from anybody. Things seem to work out that way when you go crooked. So, I was the one who took the family straight. Got a degree, went to dental school. Got a nice little practice in Brooklyn now. But those were special years. Magical in retrospect. Joes like my dad got to live out their wildest dreams right in the face of a dying Jim Crow. And yes, his deeds probably paid for some of my Meharry tuition too."

"So, this was your daddy's dream house?" Cheryl asked, punctuating her question with a wincing scan of the house's interior.

"I take it you're not sharing the dream," McRae noted.

Todd's Jeep pulled into the garage. The engine revved down, the driver's side door opened and closed. Then the trunk popped up and the golf bag hit the concrete, the irons rattling before the trunk slammed shut. This sequence of sounds echoing across the oversized garage was as familiar to Cheryl as the twelve midday *dongs* on the fake grandfather clock in the foyer. She prepared herself to answer the question she knew would be swirling around in his head the moment he'd walk through the kitchen door: "Honey, whose car is that parked out front?"

"Todd, this is Mr. McRae. His father was the original owner of the house. He was the one who had it built, in fact."

Todd lowered his golf bag from his shoulder and prepared to shake hands. McRae stood abruptly, cautiously taking in Todd's rugged military-formed frame, softened a bit by the pastel pinks on his argyle golfing sweater vest.

"At ease, Private. I'm Todd, but I suppose my Cheryl has already told you that."

Cheryl succinctly filled in all the blanks for Todd, leaving out that McRae initially scared her shitless by sneaking up to the front window, having her considering for a moment the possible need to fend off an attack.

"Hinton McRae? That was your grandfather," Todd said before settling into his favorite chair positioned under the glass dome. "Well, I'll be damned."

"You know who that is?" Cheryl asked. "Really?"

"Sure. I hear tell that Hinton McRae was a bad man in his day. Legendarily so; numbers, underground gambling and bootleg liquor—pretty much anything on the margins of the law that a black man was allowed to do in the black community was a part of his enterprise. Sweetie, you need to get out of the house. Talk to people in this town. If nothing else, you'll get an entertaining story and some sense of the history of the place." Todd took an overhead glance. "I never knew we were living in Hinton McRae's house though. Now that's really something."

"Well, you're not. Hinton was my grandfather. This house was my Dad's vision. He liked to consider himself a self-made man. Eventually a self-destroyed one too, but still."

"So what brought you here today, Mr. McRae?" Todd asked. "Just making a trip down memory lane?"

"Something like that."

Cheryl knew Todd would save his other questions for

later and that would save her from a twenty-minute narrative on how he fared on the treacherous back nine on the Army base's golf course, which, like military bureaucracy, proved no easier to tame even after becoming familiar with it. Instead, Todd pointed up to the glass dome. "What can you tell us about that? My wife here, she hates it."

"Oh, the skylight. Dad's own idea. He wanted windows everywhere to let the world know he had nothing to hide and wasn't afraid of any trigger-happy cops or jealous niggers. Excuse my language. He also wanted them to know he could see out as much as they could see in." McRae tapped his temple as if this notion were some kind of impressively shrewd maneuvering of a sharp-minded criminal. "But he needed at least one window in the house he could look out of without any constant sense of fear, you know. So he had the builders put one on top, right here in the center room so he could relax and have a clear line of sight up to God."

"A criminal and a religious man," Todd said. "Your father covering his bases, yes?"

"He actually got the idea after staying at the Hyatt in Atlanta." McRae whirled out the circumference of a circle in the air. "The one that had the glass-domed revolving bar?"

Cheryl and Todd shared a shrug. She'd gone to Atlanta for shopping at Phipps Plaza while Todd attended Falcons games, but that was it. They didn't know one Peachtree Street from another and had never spent a night in any of the city's hotels.

"I'm pretty sure it's still there. Anyway, Daddy was staying there and, as he liked to tell it, he went up to the rooftop bar and began downing gin and tonics, one right after another. And then lo and behold, the place started moving, like a slow merry-go-round and he was all of a sudden facing the other side of the city. He'd say it was the coolest, legal out-of-mind experience you could have. Spiritual, mesmerizing, reflective. Here you are on top of the world and you get to have perspective on everything around you in all directions. And the world looks back up at you and wants to be where *you* are. This is where every man wants to be, yes? Feed the basic instincts and desires of man—to be admired, envied and protected all at the same time. So, when they started in on the plans for building the house, Daddy insisted to the contractors that they put something like that glass dome right in the middle. He dreamed the center of the house could be fixed up to rotate like the hotel bar, but the skylight was as close as the builder could get within the budget they were working with. Get drunk enough though and you get the same spinning effect. The seventies were magical times. I'm just glad I got to experience some of it."

"And how did your father have his magic dome cleaned?" Cheryl asked. "Did he ever clean it?"

McRae laughed. "I don't guess I really know. Maybe Daddy hired someone from his company? The dirt, the mess, the maintenance, the cleanup, the aftermath—those are the things you don't think about when you're building and living out your dreams. But at this stage of my life, I learned that may be okay."

Todd turned to Cheryl. "Hear that, honey?"

She heard it as well as the piercing tone of dissatisfaction in his voice. Exactly what message was Todd trying to extol? Live out your dreams and don't worry about the mess? The messiness of loneliness and unfulfilling relationships?

But more likely, he was missing a truer truth: Somebody

somewhere always has to clean up after the crooks, dreamers, visionaries, and those who want to live in their shadows. Someone has to make sense of their bad or neglectful acts, assess their redemptions and decide whether or not forgiveness was merited. Someone has to advocate for the victims, before the criminal actions against them lived on as quaint stories told by strangers on lazy Saturday afternoons. The dirty glass dome had finally shed some useful light.

Just Desserts

(1992)

Wearing too-tight jeans and the same blue, green, and gold dashiki she had married in twelve years before, Sarah charged from room 107 of the Dixie Courts Motel, stinking of Virginia Slims and Seagram's gin, her heart racing, her feet bare. Rain had soaked the parking lot. She splashed in the puddles beneath her. She tried to quiet the noise by running on the balls of her feet. That was a mistake. In the night's darkness, she didn't see a section of gravel and felt it scrape an open wound on her right foot. It began to sting. Just desserts, Sarah decided. God always had a way of paying her back for the bad things she had done, and stealing money from Big Jim had to be amongst the worst. She contemplated turning around, going back to the motel room, and tossing the wallet at him. If she did, he was surely still passed out or too dazed and drunk to understand what she had done, and if he woke up, she'd tell him she took a few bucks to get a carton of smokes. He'd believe her. He didn't know her brand. If you can lie about the little things, Sarah had learned, the big lies come easier.

And even if Big Jim didn't believe her, he wouldn't care. All he'd be thinking was that he was still going to get some that night, if his limp whiskey wienie could come to life. At the bar, earlier that night, he assured Sarah it would.

"Me and you, we're going to fuck tonight, blondie," he'd said. He smiled, lowered his pointing forefinger towards Sarah's crotch, and made gunshot sounds.

She had just arrived at the bar with his cousin, Mariah-Lynn, who introduced them and excused herself to cash in some drink coupons. That was the only reason Sarah went along anyway, the promise of watered-down, half-priced strawberry daiquiris. She didn't know that eight hours later she'd be committing a felony and running in the dark on a two-lane highway, her blood and the dirty puddle water creating chemical reactions on her skin. Beneath a street light, Sarah stopped, opened her clenched fist, and looked at the scrunched cash she held in her hand. She smoothed out the bills and counted. Two fifties, a twenty, a ten, and a two. Big Jim's lucky two-dollar bill, the very one he showed off at the bar. He had kept it for years, he said. Whenever he had that two-dollar bill, no woman could resist his sex appeal, all 300-plus pounds of it. A charming little line. The foolishness amused her, his thinking that his fat ass was actually going to have her that night. Getting robbed served him right for such arrogance. God wasn't punishing her for robbing Big Jim; he was telling her next time you rip off some stupid horny bastard and run away, don't forget to put your shoes on first.

Greyhound came to mind, but God only knew when the next bus was due out there in the country. At some point, Big Jim would wake up, find his wallet missing, and maybe call the police and give them Sarah's name and description. Or maybe he wouldn't. How would he explain to some peckerwood sheriff that he had been held up by a blip of a white girl, 40 miles outside of Atlanta? Getting back to the city as soon as possible was the best thing to do.

Sarah flagged down the second car she saw on the road. A female figure sat in the passenger seat. Two strangers would feel safer than one, and the car was a late-model Toyota Camry with in-state plates, not exactly the prototypical serial killer mobile.

"Hi, y'all headed towards Atlanta?" Sarah asked as the window on the passenger side of the car lowered. She heard anxiousness in her voice. She tried it again, slower, as if her question weren't a desperate plea, just casual curiosity. "Hi. Where you folks headed? Towards Atlanta?"

The passenger was a redheaded girl, in her twenties maybe, and the driver a man, old enough to be her father. He leaned over to peer out the car window. The side of his head brushed up against the girl's tightly contained breast and she giggled.

"What's the matter? You need a ride?" the girl asked.

Sarah froze. Lying to women was harder than lying to men; women make quick deductions. Only a version of truth would be able to come out.

"I came here tonight from Atlanta. With someone. It was a mistake and I need to get back."

"You aren't hurt or anything?" the man asked. His head was still snuggled against the girl's chest, comfortable and familiar-like even in the presence of a stranger. No way was he her father. "If it's a police matter, we can take you up to the station. It's just a ways back in the other direction. If it's a police matter, we can do that for you." The man nodded, like the decision to do just that had already been made.

"No," Sarah said. "It was just a mistake to come out here. And I cut myself a little." Sarah raised her foot all the way up to the car's window and showed the couple the gash. With blood spreading, the cut appeared nastier than it actually was.

"Ew, that's looking ugly, lady," the girl said. "You better get in. We'll take you to a hospital."

The man rolled his eyes away from Sarah and turned his head towards the girl, locking a fierce gaze into her eyes. "She's right," he said finally. "Get in. Careful about getting that blood in the car though. It's not mine."

Sarah introduced herself, opened the back door, and rested across the seat with her bloody foot angled sideways, so as not to drip.

"It's Charlie's wife's car," the girl announced as they drove off down the road. "We're cheating."

"Moira!" Charlie's head shook nervously. "Pay her no mind."

"Oh, she's from out of town, Charlie, and I've just been dying to tell someone. It's my first time."

"This person you was with is not chasing you down or anything?" Charlie asked.

"Oh, no, he's dead to the world. Passed-out drunk, I mean." Sarah needed to change the subject. She couldn't sustain a lie in the weary, still-half-drunk state she was in.

"So, how long have you two been, uh, cheating?" she asked.

"Charlie here is my boss. He's a manager at a grocery store. We've worked together for over two years, but we've only been together about a month. Charlie's a slow mover." Moira giggled again. "He gets his wife's car and tells her he's

going to make night deposits, which is technically true."
Moira motioned to a large locked bank bag sitting between
her and Charlie. Sarah hadn't noticed the bag before.

"I see," Sarah said. Charlie seemed annoyed at the whole
exchange but stayed focused on the dark and winding road.

"Your guy tonight, how long have you two been
together?" Moira asked.

"About four hours," Sarah said. "Like I said, I made a big
freaking mistake. I just want to get back to Atlanta and forget
this night."

"Well, we'll take you to the hospital, but that's it," Charlie
said.

"Oh, we'll take you to the hospital *and* back to Atlanta.
We were just going to go park anyways, Charlie. This way we
can spend the time driving." Moira seemed pleased at
coming up with the plans for the night. "All we can do is ride
around and park," she said to Sarah in a confiding girl-talk
tone. "And parking is no fun, because Charlie will barely do
anything. He's scared I might get pregnant. Can you imagine
an illicit affair with no real sex? It's like not having an affair
at all."

"Sweetie, it's already late, and Mildred will be expecting
me," Charlie said. "Plus, how will I explain the extra mileage
put on her car if we drive all the way to Atlanta? She knows
the bank ain't no fifty miles away. And God forbid we get
there and something happens, like we get lost or get a flat
tire or something."

"Now you see why he's such a slow mover," Moira said.
"Such the worrywart. Takes no risks." She sniggled. "You're
such a hick sometimes, Charlie."

"Please, no hospital is necessary," Sara said, thinking of

the lies that would have to be told in an emergency room and the reports that would have to be written. "I just need some bandages to wrap this up in is all. A drugstore will be fine." "There's an urgent care clinic at the drugstore on East Hancock," Moira said, smiling and pleased with herself. "We can take you there."

Charlie carried Sara into the drugstore and quickly explained to the clinic attendant his situation. "I've got a girl, I picked her up on the highway. See, she's cut her foot—"

Sarah cut him off. "I stepped on a rock, taking out the trash. Stupid, I know, in the dark and in this weather, but we had some bad fish tonight and it really smelled the place up, so I just had to take the bones out to the garbage cans. It looks worse than it is. Can I just have some gauze to put on it? That should be fine."

Charlie's bewildered eyes danced between the bored clinic attendant and Sarah, as the fish story lingered silently in the air. Silence creates credibility, Sarah had learned. She'd done enough lying to know that. Most of those lies were told to protect Manny, now her ex-husband. Sarah fingered the collar of the dashiki—the one Manny brought back after a trip to Newark, New Jersey, and had given her to wear on their wedding day. Manny—or any reminder of him—always seemed to mystically enhance her lying technique, ever since they first met at Agnes Scott (he a campus janitor, charmer, and part-time drug dealer; she a freshman hating her choice of an all girls' college in the South).

Her foot wrapped in bandages, Sarah hobbled behind Charlie out of the drugstore and back into the car. Moira had been blasting hip hop on the radio, but quickly turned the station when Charlie got in.

"What was that 'taking out the trash' business all about, lady?" Charlie asked. "You told us some fellow brought you down here from Atlanta." He looked into the rearview mirror, waiting for an answer before starting the car.

"Nosey stores these days asking for all your personal information," Sarah said, mustering up some anger in her voice for effect. "I don't trust them any more than I trust the government. They get all into our private lives and can do God knows what with that information. It's none of their business how and why I got hurt; it's just their damn job to help fix what's wrong. My mechanic doesn't investigate the mysteries of my broken alternator, he just fixes it!"

"Amen, sister," said Moira. "What the heck happened in there?"

Charlie started the car. The engine revved loudly and the rain kicked in again. Hard, pounding drops beat down on the car.

"Let's take a drive to Atlanta, folks," Charlie said, opting for the two-lane highway instead of the interstate. It was a road Sarah was all too familiar with, as it was Manny's favorite route to Florida; fewer pesky state troopers traveled the back roads in those days. Sarah remembered the vast farms, roadside shops, and the tin-roof houses. Those trips were the best times she'd had with Manny. Country scenery seemed to bring out a softer, more introspective side of him. But even good memories of Manny slipped into bad ones. Sarah recalled the time she'd forgotten to put his bag in the car. Two hours into a trip down that very road, he found out, stopped abruptly, and threw her out, miles from anything or anyone.

"Why aren't we taking the interstate?" Sarah asked.

"This is the way I go," Charlie said. "Have been going this way for years. Guess you could say I'm resistant to change."

Sarah found out—and Moira too, for the first time—that Charlie had lived in Atlanta once, years ago, before the "hostile takeover," he said. He'd gone to Georgia Tech, when it was a school more known for budding engineers who had been valedictorians at their county public high schools, and not hot-shot New York point guards who wouldn't know a slide rule from a T-square. Ten minutes after mentioning that he'd gone there, Charlie admitted he flunked out. But that, he said, was testament to how hard it was to get a Tech degree in those days, and how his two years of studying mechanical engineering secured him a good sales position and ultimately the well-paying manager's gig at the supermarket, which he had held for over twenty years.

"What line of work you in?" Charlie asked. He said he figured Sarah might have been a teacher. But no teacher he knew would ever skip town for a one-nighter with a man she'd known for four hours.

"I've got a small business," Sarah offered. "Nothing big. I just like being out on my own."

Manny got her into the small business *business*, she being his middle-woman at Agnes Scott. It was a monopoly there and just a now-and-then thing, but she liked the feeling of satisfying demand and defying authority at the same time. Perhaps, Sarah thought, that's why she had stayed with Manny as long as she did. She liked being part of the process of something so easily successful with no long-term strategic planning, few setbacks, and completely tax-free income.

"Selling what?" Moira asked. She twisted herself around in the front seat and hung her folded arms over the headrest with childlike eagerness.

Sarah returned to her girl-talk voice. "Arts, crafts, jewelry, and things. It's not big money, but it pays the rent."

"I'd like to do that one day—own my own business. What should I sell, Charlie?" He laughed. "That's women for you. The cart before the horse. You'd need to figure out what talents you got and if there's a market for what you can offer before you go jumping up and opening a business. But that's women for you." Charlie's shushing preempted any reply from Moira. He turned up the car radio, tuning in to a late night call-in show coming in clearly out of an Atlanta station.

"Oh, no, not *him*," Moira protested.

"Hush up and you might learn something," Charlie said.

"Every one of our dates ends up this way. I am beginning to believe you like him more than you like me."

The talk-radio host was in the middle of a discourse about how the death penalty in America needed to be enacted swifter for it to truly be effective. A caller to the show said he'd heard that's the way they do it in *Arabian* countries— swift justice in public view to deter the potential criminal element from acting on their impulses.

Charlie nodded. "See, you might learn something. You agree back there, don't you?" he said, raising his voice.

Sarah rolled her eyes back and pretended to be asleep before she had to lie once more. They were too close to home for her to take the risk. Charlie turned up the radio volume even louder, and the show host talked continuously until they got to the outskirts of Atlanta.

"You've got to wake up and tell me whereabouts you live,"

Charlie said after he had passed the Atlanta city limits and the downtown high rises began to come into view. The streetlights in the city shone brightly, bathing the nearly empty highway in warm yellows and darkened golds. Sarah squinted when she opened her eyes.

"You know, you two have done more than enough; you don't have to go all the way in town," she said. "Why don't you just pull over at an all-night store or something? I'll call a cab from there."

"Don't be ridiculous, lady," Charlie said. "We've got you this far; we'll take you to your house. You do have a home, don't you?"

Sarah laughed. Charlie didn't. He stopped the car, reached back, and grabbed her jaw.

"I don't know what kind of game you're trying to pull, lady, but we've come all this way and we're going to make sure you get home safely. For your own good."

His hands and fingers smelled of vinegar and sweat. The odor was dizzying. She was only trying to protect him. But if he wanted to take her home, drive through her neighborhood at that hour, she would let him be. If something should happen to him—hick, clueless redneck with his teenaged non-loving lover—it'd serve him right for not listening to her.

In soft monotones, Sarah gave Charlie curt directions off the highway and into the city streets. Moira took in the lifeless bungalow homes that lined the way and the occasional stray figure walking along the sidewalks.

"Doesn't look so bad," Moira said.

"It's night, sweetie. The beasts are in, or hiding, ready to pounce on you at any minute. You just keep a look out."

"Two more blocks. I'm on the right."

Charlie stopped the car in front of Sarah's apartment, a three-story brick building with burglar bars lining the front and a cracked concrete pathway leading to steel doors daring easy entries.

"Good God, lady, you live *here*?" he said. "This looks like a prison!"

"My in-between place, I guess you could say."

"Lady, you need to get yourself out of this jungle. Perhaps it's rubbing off on you—coming all that way for a cheap fuck. That's pure jungle behavior, I'd say."

Sarah thanked Charlie for the ride and offered to retrieve some gas money from her apartment, hoping he'd say yes and that he hadn't noticed the imprint of Big Jim's balled-up bills stuffed in her jean pocket. "It'll be just a minute," she said.

The answering machine blinked obnoxiously in the dark of Sarah's apartment. Probably Mariah-Lynn wondering where the hell her cousin Big Jim was. Ignoring the red light, Sarah made a phone call instead.

"Manny, you up?" she asked. When they were together, he always seemed be. "I got something I need from you." She described Charlie's car, the direction she knew he would be traveling in, and the size of the bank bag in the front seat. During her days with Manny, she'd seen cash stuffed in many a paper bag. Hundreds of dollars could easily fit in a small grocery bag. Thousands, if the bills were tens and twenties.

Manny grumbled that his current lady friend could have answered the phone, but Sarah could tell that he still liked the way she cared enough to look out for him. He said he'd think about it. Sarah told him not to think too hard; it was a sure thing, and with business not being the way it used to be, she was sure he could use the money.

Sarah gathered together the cash she had taken from Big Jim and hurried back to Charlie, who stood waiting outside the car, arms crossed.

"Here you go," she said, and handed the wad to him. "It's all I have, but what you did was a really nice thing for me. The drugstore, the drive, and everything. I won't forget it."

"Well, you take care of yourself, and don't go running out of town without knowing how to get yourself back."

"Bye," Moira said. She smiled, though her face was worn and sleepy. She was a cute girl. Probably had been a cheerleader, but didn't have the grades to make it to college. What a shame she was wasting the few remaining years she had of her good looks on a married man, especially one like Charlie.

Sarah told them how to get back to the main street and waved them off. With Big Jim's money out of her pocket, she felt absolved. She called Manny again. A woman answered.

"Who is this? What do you need?" the woman asked defiantly but with no surprise in her voice. Late-night calls were to be expected at Manny's, and this woman seemed familiar with the routine.

Sarah played along. "I need to talk to Manny."

"Well, he gone out," the woman said. Sarah heard baby cries in the background. The woman didn't acknowledge them, so Sarah decided not to either.

"He's gone?"

"Yeah. He gone. Rushed out real quick. Said he had to take care of some business. Anything I can do for you?"

"No," Sarah answered. "I'm good."

Tea Time

The boy embraced the teacup as if it were a wounded bird. Rachel's stern proctoring evaluated as he put crusted lips to gold-banded brim, sipped but didn't slurp and lastly, placed the cup on a saucer. She rewarded perfection with a robotic nod, inviting a second opportunity to prove that no fluke had been witnessed; the boy could indeed politely finish off an entire six ounces of Darjeeling without dribbling all over his starched white shirt, chipping the china, or making some crude comment under his breath about nasty-tasting "white people" tea.

The boy failed on a follow-up, though—predictably—dropping the cup onto his lap, helplessly allowing it to roll down his leg and crash into a sun splash design on the floor. Rachel's lips pursed tightly as she examined shards of the cup and a sliver of tea flowing atop her waxed hardwood.

The boy nested his chin in the cove of folded arms atop the shiny dining room table, as he, Trevor, and Rachel mentally simmered over the playback of what had happened and what would happen next. Drowsy symphony music seeping from overhead speakers accompanied the silent deliberations.

"Don't worry about it," Trevor pleaded as he drove the

boy back to his home that evening. While his hands massaged a black bow-tie that had earlier choked his neck, the boy looked out the passenger window and watched the passing houses, stately brick cubes peeking through trees alongside a snaking parkway with no sidewalks. A good neighborhood tranquilized the boy. Trevor didn't want to interrupt. He and the boy did not speak again until they passed the street that divided healthy growing 401K accounts from desperate transactions occurring within check-cashing joints, sandwiched between Chinese carry-outs and cell phone stores.

"She mad?" the boy asked, his dreamy thoughts rattled by the car rumbling over a rickety patch of asphalt. "I know she mad. Yeah, she mad."

"Not mad, really. More like disappointed," Trevor offered. That was the wrong thing to say. The boy blasted an agonizing breath, which gusted over to Trevor a defeat he'd felt more than once since he agreed to this responsibility. He was too young for it, really—goodness, only twenty-eight. Trevor sometimes cursed the day he shook the hand of an old college buddy, a saintly rich white boy treading time at the Langston Hughes Public Charter School and recruiting every black name logged into his memory to be mentors, role models, father figures…he conjured up all sort of titles and euphemisms, switching up depending on his intended audience. For Trevor, the pitch actually hinted that, as penance for marrying a rich Jewish girl from Bethesda, he needed to give something back to, you know, *his* community. A year had passed since that white college buddy showed up at Trevor's door with a nine-year-old black kid who seemed like he hadn't had a decent haircut or a bath in weeks. Trevor's first outing with the boy led to a barbershop on

Good Hope Road, a gesture inspired by need instead of guilt, as a romp to Six Flags or a spree at Pentagon City Mall would have been. The cut cost only $15.

Rachel approved enthusiastically of the venture, which Trevor first brought up during morning wake-up time that was still precious stolen moments, not yet metastasized into rhythmic spousal rituals. The commitment would be good practice for raising future offspring, they decided; a test of parental skills and an assessment of their shared values—an avoided topic that surfaced during intimate moments of honesty, late-night snuggly chitchats, and post-coital reflections. Raising "Perfect Child," the name Trevor had secretly given their future baby, required consensus on questions of values and life partner goals. As she had done with law school, at the U.S. Attorney's office, as the vice president of the neighborhood association, and with her relationship with Trevor, Rachel approached the boy's presence in peak gear and off-the-chart focus. On the morning they first discussed the boy, Rachel kissed Trevor on the lips, sealing the deal with the chalky freshness of Tom's toothpaste.

"Don't worry," Trevor said to the boy. "We got thirteen of them teacups and saucers for our wedding. Just about the cheapest thing on our registry, you know. A registry, that's a list of things you put together and give to your friends to let them know all the gifts you want for getting married." Trevor laughed. "Can you imagine, telling everyone specifically what you want and they turn around and get it? No imagination is required. Ridiculous, yes?" The boy didn't respond. Trevor continued. "And I don't even like tea. Even if you don't know, you did the right thing. Thirteen's an unlucky number. Now we've got a nice round twelve. One day, maybe me and Rachel, we'll have a dinner party and invite ten people over so we can use all twelve tea cups at the same time."

Trevor reached for the boy's head. The nappy topside felt rough. The boy's hair grew like crabgrass. Instead of tea time, a visit to a barber would have been of better use of their time together, Trevor concluded as he eased the Honda onto a shadowy side street intersecting East Capitol and into a space alongside a red brick duplex apartment that, on every visit, seemed closer and closer to tipping over.

Trevor tapped on the smudged, diamond-shaped window pane in the door. "Evelyn? Evelyn?" he called out. The boy's mother wasn't home. This was not too much of a surprise, as she often seemed to be "just getting in" whenever Trevor brought the boy back. The boy reached into his shirt for a key hanging from a chain looped around his neck and opened the door with it. Trevor followed behind, holding his nose, readying his senses for the onslaught: the interlarded stench of a hair products menagerie and carpet mold. Inside the apartment, the smell proved more foul than usual. Trevor investigated. An open kitchen garbage pail revealed what looked to be the horrific aftermath of a bloody mauling: red mambo sauce covered the remains of chicken wings sitting atop a soiled baby diaper. Trevor tipped the pail's cover to close it and carefully tried to disguise his urge to vomit.

"Anybody home?" Trevor shouted and asked the boy simultaneously. He drifted through the rooms in search of an answer, thinking he'd found it on a note taped to the TV screen. Evelyn had beautiful handwriting, pleasant and dainty, that belied the known ugliness of her life: unbeatable weed habit, adhesive ex-con lovers, and four stints as a retail clerk at four different drugstores in a sixteen-month span.

"What she say?" the boy asked.

"Your momma just stepped out to get food for the baby. She'll be back."

The note didn't say that. It was no note at all, in fact. Just a list of some sort, reminders for Evelyn, wishful pledges, accented with heart shapes and cutesy underlines: *Make Ray buy diapers—not the cheap ones. Put in Application at DMV—say 'Cheryl sent you'. Winter coat for the boy—try Burlington.* Exclamation marks tailed the last line. The boy smacked his lips. He knew a lie when he heard one. Trevor folded the note, slid the paper into his pocket, and clicked on the television, a thin futuristic metallic rectangle in a room full of drab rounded corners, autumn colors, and undecorated beige walls.

"Let's wait a bit, see what's on TV."

The boy crept to the edge of the sofa, rested his head on the armrest, and soon began to snore a growly, man-of-the-house snore. Trevor called Rachel to let her know why he would be late.

Rachel withheld comments stirring within, Trevor knew. He learned, after scoping the full range of her moods during their two-year marriage, how her sentences trailed off during those conversations with mystery conclusions. He appreciated the trait, for he knew it was difficult for Rachel to sacrifice her open, blunt, take-charge self. Talking about black women always produced such self-censoring, possibly preventing the unburying of issues supposedly sealed after their first dozen dates. Badmouthing black women in front of Trevor: out of bounds.

"Maybe she got distracted or something; just lost track of time. Do you have her number? You should call her to check," Rachel proposed.

Trevor was unconvinced, but nonetheless ended the conversation there. Further speculations would only lead to nasty assumptions, tempting Rachel to violate her own rule. He tried Evelyn's cell number, given to him as a courtesy, it seemed; she never answered, always blaming her ever-shrinking allotment of minutes.

The boy woke from his nap to the steady sustained laughter of a TV audience. He seemed surprised to find Trevor still there.

"She back? She back yet?"

The eagerness seared into Trevor. The boy loved Evelyn so much, despite the funky apartment, the reported hysterical spankings in grocery store aisles, and the late-night dinners of chicken nuggets and French fries. She probably had good maternal instincts, if not the actual required skills. Trevor traded a pound of disdain for an ounce of sympathy; his various emotional accounts had become accustomed to such bargaining.

"I'm sure she'll be back soon. Maybe we should go outside to meet her, walk her home. Make sure she's safe out there. What do you say about that?"

Trevor reached for the boy, who had grown much too heavy to lift up. All those bad fast food dinners Evelyn shoved into him added more pounds than an adolescent boy needed.

"You should be on your feet," Trevor told the boy. He obliged.

They walked to the corner where the front of a convenience store jutted into the sidewalk intrusively, a construction or a marketing ruse to lure in passersby. Its welcoming fluorescent lighting had attracted a multihued and mixed night crew: three wiry black teenagers rifling through the frozen treats freezer, a jack-booted pair of National Parks policemen siphoning free coffee from a dingy one-touch machine, and an Ethiopian cab driver trading butter-toothed grins with his countryman behind the counter.

"Was she going here?" the boy asked. Trevor had bet so, and then hoped so. There was really no other place to be close by, public spaces of any kind being rare near the duplex. Evelyn was either there or had been there shortly before to satisfy her salty snack habit.

Trevor treated the boy to an apple, hardened to near-concrete by the store's arctic deli display. He leaned over the counter as he paid the clerk, whose eyes bounced between Trevor and the teenagers taking too long to decide between ice cream sandwiches or packaged ice cream cones.

"You know the boy's mother, don't you?"

The clerk nodded.

"Was she here tonight?" Trevor whispered. The boy polished the waxy apple against his shirt sleeve and took a determined sloppy bite that, for whatever reason, prompted giddy laughter from the teenagers.

The clerk responded in melodic phrasing. His job was just to be pleasant enough to assure every transaction occurred without confrontation or gunfire so as to get home safely to his wife and children. Period.

"Don't want to get into it, friend."

"It's not like that," Trevor declared, not exactly sure of the clerk's interpretation.

"Yeah, she was here earlier. With the baby child." The clerk rung up the apple, some nature snacks, and an auto magazine, an allowable gift the boy persuaded Trevor to buy. "But now she's not, friend. It's all I can tell you." The teenagers began a debating match about the best tasting flavor of ice cream—chocolate versus cookies-and-cream—that escalated to some playful shoving. The park policemen investigated reluctantly. With pointing forefingers, the clerk gestured and urged Trevor to leave before the inevitable clash.

"Let's get out of here. What do you say?"

The boy thanked Trevor for the magazine as he flipped through its pages. The boy chatted on, but Trevor wasn't paying much attention to him. He guided the boy to the car and buckled him into his seat. The two headed down East Capitol, the boy eying the magazine in the darkness and Trevor looking outside for the silhouette of an athletic woman with a baby lodged against her hip. A bus stop three lights down triggered a thought, a sign of some sort perhaps: a little yellow Funyuns bag floated away from the bus stop bench and into the street.

"What bus goes by here this time of night?"

The boy had a penchant for memorizing bus numbers and schedules and regaling Trevor with juicy urban tales of all he'd witnessed on the numbered routes that crisscrossed the city.

"Mainly the 96. It take people straight to where they want to go, so they run it all night long. It be packed most of the time too," the boy added, sounding like a confident veteran of public transit.

"Where do people want to go this time of night? On a Saturday?"

The boy considered the question. "Places that make them happy. Forget they troubles."

It was a mature assertion. Trevor and the boy compiled a list: bars and clubs, carry-outs, friends' houses in other neighborhoods.

"Show me the route," Trevor demanded. "I mean, tell me where the bus goes."

The boy didn't look up. "Just go back the way we came."

"Exactly?" The instructions seemed too simple, too coincidental. That couldn't be right. "Back towards my place?" Trevor asked, correcting himself in whispers, "Me and Rachel's place?"

"Yeah. That's the way the 96 go. Downtown. Up to U Street. Then over to Wisconsin all the way up to close to where y'all stay. That's basically the way we came, right?"

With his head immersed in the magazine, the boy melted away into a fantasy of chrome, speed, and horsepower and observing which rap moguls favored which luxury auto brands. The Capitol building appeared in the distance, the grandeur of its lit white dome juxtaposed against the closer shadowy scenes of flickering neon liquor store signs and faceless broke-back men congregating on the sidewalks. Trevor hesitated to make much of this symbolic snapshot, often talked and written about on his side of town, but rarely actually seen. Instead, he glanced into the rearview, where he saw a Metrobus inching towards a stop to pick up two figures.

"Is that the 96?"

The boy turned, looked back, and squinted at the bus's electronic signage. "Yeah, that's it. The number is like right on it. See? It's so late it's actually ahead of schedule." Trevor laughed at this clever nugget. The boy's brain functioned better than his school grades indicated and his over-analytical charter schoolteachers thought. Convinced that Evelyn's irresponsible escapade was being facilitated by an already-gone number 96, Trevor let the bus pass and followed behind.

The late-night bus filled up by the time the bus crossed the river. Public transit was for commuting, Trevor thought. Where could all these people be headed to at that time of night? Once into downtown, more passengers started to get off than get on, their post-alighting actions spotlighted, as if onstage, by the warm golden glow of street lamps. A trio of teenaged girls bounced from the bus door and immediately began prepping themselves for a night out, adjusting form-fitting jeans and primping glossy, shoulder-length hair. A lone older woman trudged down the sidewalk with a grocery cart. A workman bundled in heavy overalls plopped himself on a bench. Fifteen minutes along the 96's route, no Evelyn was in sight.

The boy looked up at Trevor. "Momma not on that bus."

"I never thought that."

"Then why we following it? All of a sudden, your car can't drive faster than the bus."

"Okay. It was just a wild guess that she might be somewhere along the route. I don't know what to do." Within this honest pronouncement, an uncertainty grew. Trevor tried calling Evelyn again and still got no answer. "I can take you back to our place for now."

The boy's concerned expression intensified; he seemed more worried about facing Rachel than he did the whereabouts of his own mother. Brave head nods shook off any clinging apprehension.

"That makes sense, I guess. We're halfway there anyway."

Trevor let the boy make the decision again. He scolded himself—that wasn't good parenting. But in moments of crisis, the boy seemed to have more calm than Trevor did. At least the boy didn't fear the consequence of his decisions, because he had little to lose or gain. Trevor rubbed the boy's head, realizing that was the only gesture of affection he'd ever offered. This time though, the boy scowled and turned his eyes back down to the car magazine. Trevor sped past the 96 and headed back to his home.

A blinding motion light over the doorstep greeted their arrival. Behind curtain sheers—a cultural compromise Rachel agreed upon—Trevor and the boy saw two figures sharing conversation.

"Momma!" the boy said, reaching for the doorknob and thrusting the door open. He rushed to Evelyn, nearly toppling her track-star frame as she sat straddling a dining room chair, her bare feet clawing the chair's rungs. The baby slept soundly on Evelyn's shoulder. The boy hugged Evelyn tight and, in the process, woke his baby sister who responded with an indifferent yawn.

"Boy's never been so happy to see me!" Evelyn said.

"Why you here, Momma? What you doing at Trevor house?"

"We were worried," Trevor explained. "When you weren't home, I got concerned. We tried calling multiple times.

Everything okay?" Though Trevor spoke to Evelyn, his eyes were on Rachel, her face cherry tomato-red and perspiring.

"Everything's fine," Rachel confirmed. "I kept trying to call you too."

Trevor apologized. "Sorry baby. We were so focused on finding Evelyn."

"That's okay, sweetie. It gave us a minute to talk. This was our first time meeting, you know. We're just finishing off the tea from earlier. And talking."

"The boy was so excited today, dressing himself this morning in that outfit," Evelyn said. "I just had to come see what y'all was up to with him. I expected him to be here a little longer and thought I would drop by and pick him up, save you a trip all the way to Southeast. But I didn't know y'all would have my boy playing with tea sets." Evelyn laughed. "I don't know about all that. But I suppose nothing wrong with it though, since y'all was celebrating."

Trevor grazed behind Rachel and caressed her neck as he took a seat at the dining room table. She reached for his hand and squeezed it, seeming to not want to let go.

"Celebrating?" Trevor asked.

"Yes. Your wife here tells me the good news. That you two are expecting! I was just giving her the 4-1-1 on how it's going to be during the pregnancy and then when the real work begins after that baby come out. This little one has been a challenge." Evelyn patted the baby on her back. The challenging baby stretched and yawned again, unimpressed and unperturbed by the new surroundings.

"Y'all having a baby?" the boy asked. His lips trembled.

Evelyn laughed. "Girl, I knew it as soon as I walked in and

saw your face getting all red and sweaty like that. With your hormones acting crazy, that's how it's going to be for the rest of your term."

The boy asked again. "Y'all having a baby?" Trevor turned to Rachel, waiting for the answer.

"Well, soon. We aren't really telling people just yet," Rachel said to the boy. "But I thought it was important to tell your mother here why Trevor won't be spending as much time with you as he has been."

Trevor slipped into silence as Rachel's grip grew tighter and tighter.

"I understand," Evelyn said, before detailing all that Trevor had done for the boy. "He can never stop talking about the trips to the library, all the downtown museums and other places you took him. It was a good thing you done, Trevor. Every little bit helps. And it was more than his real daddy could ever come up with." Evelyn suctioned in her bottom lip, probably blocking her tongue from pinpointing a more apt descriptor than "real daddy" in front of the boy. She gave the boy a little push. "Go on over there and tell Trevor thank you for all he's done."

"I was glad to do it," Trevor said. "He is such a smart young man; an absolute gentleman in the making." Trevor wanted to touch the boy, do something more than rub his head. Maybe hug him in earnest, tell him that he would still keep in touch. But the boy inched backwards into the embrace of his mother, she fully enveloped with the love of her children. Instead, Trevor rubbed Rachel's heaving belly. "So tell us, Evelyn, what all can we expect when we have our child?" Trevor asked. "We want to be really good parents. Just like you."

Dates for Kreeger

Graduate degrees in public policy aren't usually associated with prodigies, but Kreeger proved to be certifiable after he breezed through undergrad and the Kennedy School before his twenty-second birthday. From there, he took a job with the city of Norfolk. Bergen County had offered fifteen grand more and threw in the kind of perks unique to zip codes with high concentrations of millionaires—free health club memberships and access to county-owned cars. But Norfolk had its own advantage: lots and lots of men in uniform.

The administrative assistants in the Norfolk city manager's office collectively shook their heads when Kreeger splayed year-old copies of *Men's Health* across his desk, dropping the penultimate hint that he was, as rumored, off-limits not because he was some snobby Martha's Vineyard vacationer dripping with inaccessible fineness, but because... well, he was living in some sort of purgatory of a sexual kind, and needed to figure some things out.

Kreeger had learned in college that he didn't have the gumption to just come out and say *it* directly, especially when black women were in the audience mix; he'd let them assume and guess and gossip about some supposed fondness for fashion, museum openings, celebrity hairstyles, and reality drama. Over time, he could maybe share tears about no-account men and the perils of growing up with low self-esteem in a world that didn't value their kind of beauty and sass. Later, he could possibly drop details about his church choir and the challenge to whip them into shape for a gospel extravaganza just six months away. Stoic, tight-lipped, non-musical, and a bad dresser, Kreeger ultimately had none of that to offer. So he just waited until the questions came bluntly, his canned answers always at the ready.

That's kind of personal.

For now, I'm just single.

In Norfolk, at work, the questions didn't come. All parties reached a whispered conclusion. Afterwards, the admins became Kreeger's chief allies in the underground battle against the office Holy Holies, a ring of righteous Jesus-talkers who turned their sunburned noses up high—at Ivy League degrees, long work days, new ideas, and homos, confirmed or not.

"It's all right, baby," LaDonna said between conciliatory hugs, rubbing her sweaty balloon chest all up in Kreeger's face. She was the chairperson of the administrative assistant consortium. "They jealous." She sucked her teeth and rolled her eyes in a way she probably thought Kreeger should have been doing himself. Instead, he just smiled a thin smile of cautious appreciation for her concern.

Kreeger headed home each evening to the garden apartment he rented in Virginia Beach, Norfolk's sister city—if that sister were a pious, sprawling, God-fearing seaside slacker. He had chosen a place close enough to the ocean to smell salt air from the balcony and take spontaneous midnight strolls on the boardwalk. There, on the loneliest of nights, Kreeger mulled over the roads not taken. Perhaps he should have heeded his advisor's advice and aimed for a Ph.D. in political science, a field—Kreeger had been told over and over—woefully in need of black students with fine minds. Amidst riffing on new thinking and dynamics and paradigm shifts and academic social activism and the fulfilling responsibilities of public intellectualism, Kreeger knew the advisor was just trying to hit on him, desperately wanting a star pupil to stay in Cambridge and study more than black socio-political movements. Or maybe he should have listened to the parents, using his pretty darn good LSAT scores as a ticket to a "T-14" law school, the last resort of his undergrad poli-sci classmates suffering from chronic overachievement. Or he should have followed the first and last man who'd called him 'lover,' that doughy and shy older Italian-American campus cop who dreamed of retiring early and shacking up in the woods of Vermont. Black and gay in the backwoods of Vermont? That answered itself.

So Norfolk it was. The quest for rugged relationship experimentalists in uniforms quickly proved intimidating and futile; the military boys, they stuck to their own kind. But the Tidewater seascapes impressed Kreeger, as did the palpable confused psychology of a place that seemed evenly poor and rich, black and white, traditional and offbeat, downtown white collar and dockside working class, nebulously Mid-Atlantic and downright Southern, providing easy access to well-seasoned fried chicken, butter-laden cakes and sweetened tea. Kreeger fashioned a secret tagline for his new city—*Norfolk: a good place to be a little paradoxical.*

"What exactly do you do?" one pitiful flirt asked during

that first venture into the edge of a revitalizing neighborhood with a lonely gay bar, identified discreetly with a rainbow sticker affixed to a single window pane on the front door. The questioner had already spilled that he taught philosophy and religion at Old Dominion—*if only the parents knew*—but pined for living out his true passion by doing research at a particular progressive think-tank up in D.C. Kreeger wondered why he always met the ones wanting to be somewhere other than where they were. What did attracting the nomadic type say about him? Accompanying each round of drinks, anecdotes warned of the difficulty of being a homosexual, intellectual, black male in *the 757*, the prideful area code and shorthand for the municipalities wandering across the Tidewater. The professor wanted to sleep with him—Kreeger could tell—but the poor old guy didn't know how to transition from his philosophical musings and tales of woe to anything remotely attractive or sensual, to say nothing of boldly lusty.

So Kreeger focused on work after that horrible night. Weeks of nothing social. The evenings' activities rotated around home, the beach and solo workout sessions in the apartment gym. And then he met Larry.

Larry had been sent over from the city's public relations department to do an interview about a ten-year-old land use plan Kreeger himself had just begun to dust off. Larry wore no socks and white loafers to the meeting. He introduced himself as a "fish out of water" but was diligently dedicated to learning and understanding the planning and policy mumbo-jumbo that would come his way during the interview.

"You like seafood?" Larry finally asked in response to what must have been a blank stare or an incoherent response to some query. Kreeger really hadn't gotten beyond that "fish out of water" comment.

"You look hungry. You like seafood? I know a great place if you do. We can knock this discussion out over a good meal somewhere versus having it amidst uninspiring government-issued office furniture."

Kreeger and Larry sat waterside on a cool autumn evening. Heat lamps overhead made Larry's fair hair seem shinier and blonder. His looks hinted at potential cuteness, like a movie star's before-famous photos. Larry kept a notepad and his laptop close by, but didn't use either. Instead, he did a lot of talking, telling Kreeger of his journey from a real-life Mayberry in North Carolina and up the coast to Norfolk, lamenting that he hadn't gone further up the Eastern Seaboard or down to Atlanta because he'd heard great things about the lifestyle there.

Lifestyle. Kreeger pondered over that one while chewing bites of catfish, fried crispy. The evening ended with Larry admitting that he'd gotten absolutely no work done, what with the three pinot grigios flooding his system. He would need to set up a third meeting to actually talk about land abuse or toxic waste or the greening of Norfolk or whatever the original topic was. Larry pulled out a smartphone and deftly worked its face. He looked for an open spot in his calendar, its time slots filled densely with colored blocks, night and day. "I'll see if I can squeeze you in," he said, finally.

"You called me, remember?" said Kreeger, fueled by a couple of Manhattans poorly made by an overworked Latino busboy-slash-bartender.

Larry reached over to grab the bill then lightly brushed away Kreeger's hand. "I got this," Larry said. "Don't worry.

This will be good for your career here. Be patient, friend. We all have to be patient in Norfolk."

What did he know? He didn't even take the time to do his land use homework to write a stupid city press release. He probably wanted Kreeger to just come out and write the thing for him. It was all a "playing hard to get" move, Kreeger realized. He could do better.

"Like you needed him," LaDonna said at the retelling of the encounter. She was bent over and fishing for extra change out the soda machine in the kitchen at work. Kreeger stood behind her, watching the futility of her effort. "He ain't got nothing you want. Believe me, I've seen them cheap, scuffed-up, twenty-dollar faggoty Payless shoes he be wearing." She turned and patted Kreeger on his shoulder. "Oh, no offense or nothing, baby."

"None taken."

LaDonna gave up, resigned that she would have to pay for her afternoon Doritos with her own money, which she did. She pierced the small bag and daintily picked out a large chip, holding it aloft in the air before making her next point, "In all my days, I just ain't never seen it work. A white boy and a black man. Eventually, they turn out to be just that, a *White Man*—capital W, capital M—wanting to make all the rules, dictating every last living part of your relationship. Making you play the game on their terms. Their natural human cultural inclination just emerges, battling hard against the other side of their submissive feminine personality. With that kind of conflict going on in their heads, when you think about it, being a gay white man has to be the hardest existence in the world."

LaDonna rejected her theory pretty quickly. She and Kreeger agreed that it was the black woman who was the world's mule and the black male homosexual the fly circling the mule's ass. She departed, promising she would work her network of friends, co-workers and family members to find Kreeger a real date with a respectable, intellectual, financially stable *black* man—the gay version of the archetype she herself could not find.

Kreeger wouldn't have to wait for LaDonna's fix-up. While standing in line at the Food Lion grocery store and skimming the alternative weekly, an advertisement headline caught his eye: "Knowing Thyself: A Testimonial of Learning How to Be In The Life. One Black Man's Journey." The author would be signing the next day at the Barnes & Noble.

An older woman with the look of a retired librarian preemptively greeted Kreeger at the door of the bookstore and promptly directed him to the back corner, where a line had formed to enter a roped-off area. It felt a bit like a quarantined cell so as to protect the kids in the children's section from a gathering of perverts "in the life." The author seemed unfazed, sporting a gorgeous smile and an ultra-tailored pinstripe suit torn from the pages of GQ. He looked out of place in a chain bookstore filled with pasty moms in jeans and beer-bellied dads in Saturday cargo pants.

"Greetings, gentlemen," the author finally said from a podium, and the crowd of twenty-five or so grew quiet. "And lady," he added, though there were actually three women present. The audience laughed at his joke, but awkwardly so.

The author began his presentation with a minute of meditative silence before embarking on a rehearsed telling of when he first *knew*. Every time Kreeger heard such stories, they always seemed to start with a fascination of the clothes in a mother's closet or the discovery of a sister's Barbie dolls or weird feelings manifesting at the sight of a certain boy. This author, though, said his moments trickled out subtly during his adolescence and his early teen years. Okay, yes, he had a mild crush on the 9th grade quarterback, but "The Voices" in his head convinced him that those feelings were inconclusive, untrue. "Now, fast forward a dozen and two years and I am writing books helping others fight those voices that shout only self-loathing, negativity, and fear." Kreeger applauded with the other men in the audience, many offering synchronous knowing head nods.

The author wound through his labored reading of an excerpt of his book and as tears began to fall in the audience, Kreeger's academic skepticism surfaced—this guy was no psychologist, so his insights weren't rooted in anything a scientist could or would want to validate. But he had a soothing voice and a regular story to tell, one that would sound much like Kreeger's own if he were ever willing to share. So Kreeger decided to buy the book, but probably not read it—at least not right away.

The author concluded with an air of relief. An appreciative standing ovation followed. The bookstore staff hustled to move the event to its next phase, directing the author to a table and instructing those who had paid for their books to get in line for the signing. After purchasing his copy, Kreeger eased into line, ambling quietly behind a chatty couple so absurdly dramatic in their praise for the book that it almost made him want to bail. But then the man who would be Kreeger's third Tidewater date tapped him on the shoulder from behind.

"So, what did you think?"

Kreeger turned and met a pair of square pecs hiding behind a fresh Navy T-shirt. The guy lowered himself and made eye contact. He introduced himself as Kurt. He fumbled the author's book to shake Kreeger's hand, so no poised athlete was he, just a guy who spent too much time in the gym.

"It was good. Interesting," Kreeger answered. "I learned some things."

Kurt pointed at the author, accepting more gushing silly praise and laughing too loudly. "You learned some things about him or yourself?"

"Yes, *know thyself.* Right. Guess I'll have to actually read the book to find out."

"You can skip the reading and I can give the short course," Kurt said. More cryptic language. Must be a Southern thing, Kreeger surmised; white or black, in or out, these boys from the South learn to cloak their lifestyle in colorful turns of phrases and jokey charm to mask the pain and shame. They find solace in being just quirky and odd, hoping, at worst, that a swishy boy with a funny voice equates to nothing more harmful than a batty old aunt spouting nonsensical aphorisms. Or perhaps it was all a learned mechanism for deflection and confusion, insurance language to prevent getting the crap beat out of you. Kurt chatted on intelligently about whether these kinds of books actually helped black gay men or perpetuated a kind of victim's posture, charting a sad, lifelong course of endless justification and wasted reflection instead of just a damn celebration of being. "That's why, usually, I just stick to porn when I need any self-affirmation," Kurt joked. Kreeger smiled a nervous smile. All that easy wit seemed odd coming from chiseled chocolate granite.

But Kreeger shared more. He told Kurt about his brief time in Norfolk and the challenges of a work project, an assessment of all the sustainability studies that had been done for the city in the last few years—his "It's not easy making Norfolk green" punchline fell flat. Then he went backwards, uncapping a life summary, strategically tossing in those Ivy degrees and teen years filled with overachievement and "good works." Kurt then shared that he was from Michigan, an engineer and a gearhead—not actually in the military. But since many in Norfolk always seemed to assume, he sometimes played along.

When they reached the front of the line, the author greeted Kurt and Kreeger jointly. Then he leaned back in his chair and paused to consider, it seemed, the feasibility that the two were a couple.

"And who should I make *yours* out to?" the author asked Kreeger, fishing for clues. Kreeger responded instinctively by spelling out his name.

"And yours, sir?"

"Kurt with a 'K.'"

"K and K? Sounds like the perfect union," the author joked.

"Kurt with a K?" Kreeger asked. "That's a first for me."

"There's a first time for everything," Kurt said.

That was good flirting, Kreeger decided—banal, clever, not too forced. And then, the invite.

"After we're done here, you want to…"

Kreeger sucked in a breath, fearing that Kurt would want to hit up the same sort of lame bar scene where he encountered the sad professor, or worse, some cruddy vacationer's spot on the beach, where the down-low crowd lived out weekend fantasies. Kurt asked his question again. This time, Kreeger found his calm ears. The offer was to check out his sports car, one with a series of masculine-sounding letters and numbers appended to its brand name. *MXT? XTZ?* For compact-car driving Kreeger, it failed to impress. But he had long ago learned the art of interest-feigning, mixing head tilts with probing open-ended follow-up lines.

With their signed copies of *Know Thyself,* Kreeger and Kurt marched out the door of the bookstore and into the parking lot of the shopping center. Kreeger followed behind until Kurt egged him to take the lead and challenged him to find the car, which proved not too difficult in a sea of SUVs, trucks, and practical sedans.

Kurt's car had fat tires and a sloping bright yellow body. "That one over there?"

"Ding, ding, we have a winner," Kurt said. He announced its feature list like a commercial spokesperson. His face blossomed as he talked about the engine and the great deal he got, scheming the dealer for add-ons and extras. *Men and their cars.* Kreeger would never understand, but when Kurt offered a ride along the ocean highway, adventure awaited.

"Top down or up," Kurt joked as he started the engine. It was too cold to have the top down, so it was definitely a joke or more code. When Kurt turned the key in the ignition, the muscles along his arm flexed, transforming into even harder concrete. "How do you like that sound?"

"Let's just see what this baby can do," Kreeger said, conjuring up some tenor in his voice he had not heard since pretending to care about rivalry football games in college. The drive was nice though, breezing along Shore Drive with the autumn air slipping through half-open windows. Kurt maneuvered with ease, taking complete control of his machine. Kreeger usually felt vulnerable in cars, like a caterpillar in a cocoon waiting to be smashed by some monstrous kid playing God. With Kurt in the driver's seat, that feeling seeped away. *Men and their cars.* Kreeger thought he began to understand.

The highway winded into a leafy area along the northern shore. Kurt slowed down and turned into the entrance of a dock.

"Where are we going?"

"Thought you might like to check out my boat."

"You sure you aren't Navy?" Kreeger joked.

"No. Just a wannabe."

Kurt guided Kreeger onto the deck of the boat, a sleek little pleasure cruiser; the *Dream Hunter* it had been named. Kurt unlocked a cooler and grabbed a couple of beers, handing one to Kreeger who attempted to find his sea legs as he walked to a rear seat on deck. Kurt took the seat beside him, plopping his frame down as if welding himself in for a long evening. The boat rocked easily in response. They clicked beer bottles and toasted.

"To new friends," Kreeger said nervously.

"To finding and hunting down your dreams," Kurt responded.

They clicked bottles again and turned their gazes to the

sea, where the approaching dusk created an almost indecipherable horizon line.

"How did *you* know?" Kreeger asked, breaking a silence.

Kurt let loose a broad smile. "Certainly not because I wanted to put on my mom's funky pantyhose. I've always connected with people. I don't need labels for those connections. If the world feels the need to place that connection in a particular bucket, then so be it." Kurt nodded and pointed to the horizon. "I'll be off hunting my dreams. We only get so much time in this realm; why waste it with angst and analysis like your author friend back there?"

"Then why did you go to the reading in the first place?" Kreeger asked.

Kurt grabbed Kreeger's free hand. "Just connecting, my man. Just connecting. To connect though, you've got to get out there and not put others in a box you yourself don't want to be in. Take charge of your destiny, friend. What are you waiting for? What are you hungry for in a relationship or life? You can't just place yourself situationally as you've done with everything else in your life. The right schools and the right job choices that come landing in your lap. You've got to act. What are you dreaming about every day?"

Kreeger didn't know the answer to that one; his education had failed him, and he had no canned responses in either his head or his gut. He wanted to feel this Kurt though. Feel that energy he was giving off.

"Stick with me. I will introduce you to some folks. With the right person in your life, you may be able find your dream too."

A door opened from the deck floor. Kreeger had not

noticed it was there. Stretched arms and hands emerged from the portal and a yawning, rail-thin figure made its way up. The stretching arms morphed into balletic dance moves across the deck.

"You cheating on me again, Kurt?" the man asked.

"You know me," Kurt said. "I am constantly being forced to run to the arms of others, since I don't get enough affection at home."

The boat man shook his head and gave Kurt a playful tap on the hand then a lazy kiss on the cheek. Kurt introduced Kreeger as a new friend, new in town, and then introduced the boat man as his partner, but said the word in a way that sounded strange to Kreeger's ears. "*My pardnah.*" They created something familial and unique; something that allowed Kurt to lead Kreeger on, perhaps as a joke or an adventure. Kreeger wanted to lay a punch right into Kurt's abdomen, but that surely wouldn't end well.

"We'll have to work on you, Mr. Kreeger," the partner said, resting his face in his hands while eying Kreeger intently, as if to ponder a correct course of action. He had joined Kurt and Kreeger, wedging his way into a corner seat that positioned him as the conversation lead. "So, what kind of fellows do you like, sir?" he asked Kreeger.

Kreeger's throat tightened, his stomach shriveled. Before he could label himself, identify an appropriate target and act, he knew he had to first learn the rules of this game.

Crystal Lake

My father's fraternity chapter held its annual family picnic at Crystal Lake, a brown haven for mosquitoes surrounded by a mass of weeds, red clay, and a few intimidating signs warning against swimming. It was located on an Army base just twenty minutes outside town, but far enough away to make it feel remote and exotic. Beside the lake, growing from the weeds, there stood a pavilion that in a former life had been a clapboard barrack, a vestige of World War II days when the base was a camp, housing thousands of soldiers waiting their turn to fight.

For the picnics, the fraternity families would stake out prime spots under the pavilion, trying in vain to beat the oppressive August weather worsened by the heat of the grills, where turkey dogs and burger patties for the kids cooked alongside chicken and slabs of ribs for the parents. Before the eating began, some responsible adult would inevitably wave the curious among us kids away from the lake—"*If you fall in, I'm not coming to getcha!*"—and onto the sizzling hot playground equipment—so hot it would redden the backs of my buttermilk thighs. If someone remembered to bring a ball, we'd opt to play dodgeball or volleyball in a playground clearing landscaped with sparkling white beach sand that contrasted sharply with the hardened Georgia clay nearby. The adults, however, provided the real entertainment for us kids. Among our favorites were the Lynams—she, a large woman always professing the virtues of her diets while planted before mounds of potato salad and pork and beans, and he, a rickety diabetic who used cuss words, told dirty jokes, and whose left hand stayed glued to cans of Miller Lite.

I remember when I was nine, attending my eighth picnic in 1979. It was Mr. Lynam who greeted my family and me as we poured out of our station wagon. As he always did, he called me by my older brother's name.

"Terry? Is that you? How's my boy Terry?"

"Doing fine," I answered shyly, thinking it improper to correct a grown man, but okay to mock the gravel in his voice. Mrs. Lynam tried to remind her husband of my actual name, but he chose not to hear her.

"You enjoying yourself, Terry?" Mr. Lynam asked me. He wasn't a tall man, but he bent over, emphasizing with grunts the effort it took to talk to a little kid.

Yes," I answered, even though I had just arrived and I hadn't yet had the chance to do anything to either enjoy or not enjoy.

"Good, good, because we do this for the kids." Mr. Lynam reared back and took a long chug of his beer. He shook the can. "Looks like I'm on empty. Go on and have some fun with the rest of them knuckleheaded bastards." Mr. Lynam laughed and gently pushed me towards the playground where a huddle of boys stood listening intently to Alex Cunningham, a showboat of a kid who had the aura of a grown man before reaching puberty.

Most of us were teachers' children. For our parents and

us, Crystal Lake was last call, a final chance to squeeze an ounce of fun out of the too-short summer vacation months. Alex, though, was different. His father was an Army colonel, twelve months a year, every day, all day long. And while we spent our summers watching TV and playing games in the air-conditioned cool of our split-levels, Alex was away in camps, the Cub Scout kinds with no girls, 7:00 a.m. wake-up calls and long, boring nature hikes that resulted in bouts with poison ivy. For the Cunningham kids, the scouts was a junior-level Army of sorts, a first stop on the military train before JROTC in high school, the ROTC in college, and a life of discipline and uniformity. The picnics at Crystal Lake were R&R for Alex, a break from battling plants, toads, and leeches on the front line. Standing there in an olive green short set, Alex held court, telling about the garden snake he found and cut to pieces with his pocketknife earlier that summer at a camp. He pulled out the knife and held it up for inspection. His mother made him clean the snake blood off, he said; otherwise, we would have seen blood right there, dried up and encrusted on the knife's blade.

"You're a liar," I announced as I arrived and penetrated the circle. Alex was a lifelong braggart, always turning his boyish adventures into war stores.

"What would you know?" Alex said. "You wouldn't know anything about camp because you've never been."

"Liar!"

"Asshole!"

"Fag!"

"Double fag!"

Back and forth we went, with the kids edging us closer to one another and hoping our verbal jabs would spawn a fistfight, or at least a worthwhile shoving match. Alex was bigger than me and he did have a knife on him, so I hoped we'd only get as far as a few shoulder taps before some adult would see the commotion and separate the two of us.

"The language, boys. Watch the language!" I heard a saving voice coming from outside the circle. It belonged to Captain Scott, one of the youngest men in the fraternity. Like Alex's father, he was all Army—fit, clean-shaven, tight pants— except he was not married. A boy accompanied him, one about my own age at the time. "Now, if you all can just stop this horseplay, I'd like to introduce you to somebody," Captain Scott said.

Everyone turned to face the new boy who looked over us, one by one. We looked him over too, staring him down in unison. His face was dusky, his hair nappy, and a long-healed scar spanned the side of his cheek. His eyes sank deeply into his face. His clothes were worn out and old, but he did have on a pair of Chuck Taylor All Star tennis shoes, white ones, clean and looking brand new. The sneakers even eluded the dusty clay on the path leading to the playground. I saw the boy's toes wiggling inside the shoes as if he were just getting used to them or could not believe they were really on his feet.

"This here is Luwann, boys. He's my little brother," Captain Scott said, his voice fixed in a staccato 'captain's orders' mode.

My eyes rose from the boy's face up to Captain Scott's smooth, milky complexion and the neat pattern of freckles that spread across his nose and cheeks.

"Now, he's not my *blood* brother," Captain Scott clarified. "But we're real close, and I want you to treat him like one of the regulars." We all shook hands with the boy as Captain

Scott directed us to do. Luwann joined our circle. Questions whirled around the poor kid.

"What school you go to?"

"Where you stay?"

"What's your name? Luwanna?"

"Ain't that a girl's name?"

"How you know Captain Scott?"

"Where you get them bad-assed All Stars from?"

"Captain Scott, he a fag? Do he be feeling on you?"

Finally able to answer at least one question, Luwann said he lived in Sunrise Homes, which one of the kids whispered was the bad projects on the east side of town. He went to Anderson Elementary where Mrs. Lynam taught. He pointed her out in the distance; she waved back at him in recognition. Luwann stuttered before answering any more questions then laughed them off nervously, even as Alex prodded. Then, Alex remembered it was my ass he was to be kicking and humiliating and not some shy kid from the projects happy to be wearing new sneakers. Alex gave me a quick karate chop, square into my upper chest. The gathered boys oohed and aahed, mimicked the blow, and made squealing Bruce Lee noises as the pain seeped slowly down into my body.

"Still say I'm a liar?" Alex said. His hand readied for another karate chop, this time one aimed for my ribs.

Captain Scott saw him ready to strike. "Save that for someone your own size, Cunningham!"

I let out a huge sigh as all the boys began to disperse. All except Luwann, who stood in front me, head bowed, not knowing where to go or what to do. "They've got grape sodas over there in that barrel," I managed to say over the pain in my chest. "You want one, Luwann?"

"Welch's? NuGrape?" Luwann's eyes blossomed.

"No, store brand, but what they got is all right; almost as good as the real stuff." As I led Luwann to the drink barrel, we heard Alex behind us bragging that his red karate belt made it unfair to fight me anyway, and that his father way outranked that sissy Captain Scott and could make him do pushups anytime, anyplace.

"What rank your daddy is?" Luwann asked me.

"Rank? My dad's not in the Army. He hates the Army! Says it brainwashes people," I said. Luwann appeared confused, but I didn't know where to begin or how far back I needed to go. "This is a fraternity see, not the Army," I said. "We're just here on post because Alex's daddy is a colonel, and they let him use this place for free."

"Fraternity?" Luwann stretched out the word, carefully making sure his pronunciation matched mine.

"Yeah. See, it's like a club. Men have to join them when they go to college," I explained. "The ladies have their own clubs, they're called sororities. After college, they still get together sometimes and have meetings, parties, and this." I opened my arms wide, as if to collect the lake, the barrack pavilion, the barbecues, all the gathered families, and—in a way—life as I had known it up to that point. It was a warm and comfortable embrace, even with pain pulsing in my chest.

We stopped and fished for grape sodas in the icy waters of the barrel, but came up empty. Grape always went first. Only cans of the no-name cola were left.

"Those are some cool All Stars," I said. "How did you get them?"

I waited anxiously for the story, and could even hear

myself repeating it before Luwann could tell me. He stole them, from the back of a department store truck. Or they were a once-a-year gift from some sorry out-of-town dad, who probably stole them himself. Or I'd get all the details on how Captain Scott cruised streets in the ghetto all night long, in search of one gangly shy boy in need of a father figure in his pitiful role model-less life. How he'd take those boys to his house and do God knows what to them. And how he'd buy them off with a brand new pair of high-top Chuck Taylor All Stars, making them the envy of all the project kids who lived on the east side.

I was right. Captain Scott did buy the shoes—that day, in fact. But if there was more to the story, Luwann wasn't sharing.

"He cool. He buy me things" was all I got.

Luwann took a long, satisfying sip of the cola, which made me squeamish since I knew how nasty it was. In the distance, I could see Captain Scott talking with my father, smiling and pointing at me and Luwann. It had been five minutes and he'd already made me and this kid out to be best pals. He seemed proud, standing there as if admiring something he'd just built with his own hands. I wanted out of the creepy and happy picture Captain Scott was painting, so I offered to show Luwann around the lake. As we walked, I told him things I had seen there before—alligators, turtles—lying in an attempt to make Crystal Lake seem like the exotic coastal wetlands it resembled. All we found when we got to the lake's edge were mosquitoes and one of the "No Swimming" signs posted by the Army Corp of Engineers. They had allowed swimming in the past; I'd seen happy, grinning faces splashing around in old pictures. But after a kid had drowned in the sixties, swimming was banned. Everyone said the kid who died was a "champion swimmer" too, and if he couldn't survive Crystal Lake, no one could. I looked over the lake every year, examined it closely, trying to imagine how that kid could have drowned in those lifeless waters.

"I believe it was alligators," I told Luwann. "One snapped his leg and took him under." I clapped my hands together like a shutting mouth. As I pondered the alligator theory, Luwann bent over to brush off some lakeside mud bold enough to finally muss up his Chuck Taylor's. The reddish slime had spread all over the shoes, some of it reaching the star emblem that adorned the upper sides of the high tops. He cursed himself for allowing it to happen, especially before anyone in his neighborhood got to see them fresh and clean.

"Clean them up now," I offered apologetically, feeling guilty that I was the one who led him to the mud. "That way, the dirt won't settle in and you can just throw them in the washing machine later then clean the star with some Formula 409."

"We ain't got a washing machine! No Formula 409." Luwann's face contorted in frustration.

"Well, take them off and wash them, here in the lake."

For some reason, Luwann listened to me tell him to wash his shoes in the brown waters of Crystal Lake. Desperation, I suppose. He carefully untied the sneakers, took the laces all the way off, and put them in his pockets. He knelt at the edge of the lake, wet two fingers, and began scrubbing the canvas part of one shoe, first carefully then with vigor. It was a futile effort; the red clay mud seemed to be setting in deeper and deeper.

"Stop. That's not going to work," I said. "I'll go find something better. A brush maybe. They might have one around here, you know, for cleaning up the grills later."

Luwann insisted on continuing his scrubbing, repeating my own words about not wanting to let the mud settle in. Under his breath, he again cursed the mud, the sneakers, and the picnic itself.

"God, they're just sneakers, man, even if they are All Stars," I said. Luwann returned a half-bemused, half-angered look.

"Okay, okay," I said. "Don't do anything else. I'll be back."

Luwann, kneeling as if in prayer, waited as I went to go find a brush.

"Where's Luwann. Everything okay out there?" Captain Scott asked me when I reached the pavilion. I explained to him about the shoes. "You left him by the lake alone?" he asked.

Mr. Lynam, listening in nearby, turned, squinted, and looked towards the lake. "I see him; his little pea head sticking up out there. He all right," he said. "But that boy didn't look like no Mike Spitz though. You brought him, Captain, you the one need to be over there watching him."

Captain Scott sighed in agreement. He marched towards the lake with me and Mr. Lynam behind him. In a straight line, we headed for Luwann, still hunkering over the lake's edge. We saw him raise one shoe, high above his head, and hurl it towards the lake. The shoe arced high, turning over once in mid-air before dropping into the lake, splashing, quickly disappearing beneath the surface, then floating back to the top, its rubber sole facing up.

"What did you do that for? Do you know how much those

shoes cost?" Captain Scott said, standing directly above Luwann. "Frustration's no excuse. Now go get that shoe."

"Don't make the boy do that, Captain," Mr. Lynam said. "You don't know what's in that water."

"It's not so deep there," Captain Scott said. He snapped off a low-hanging branch from a tree and gave it to Luwann. "Here, use this. Go on out there and get that shoe back. It'll teach you to appreciate the things people give to you."

Other parents and children, including Alex's father and mine, heard Luwann's crying, saw us there, and began to gather. Alex offered to retrieve the shoe, announcing that he had completed a mile swim in camp, one of only three kids in the whole county to do so.

"No, this is a lesson that needs to be taught. Nothing will happen," Captain Scott said. "You can't coddle these boys. I'll watch him."

Luwann eyed the spot in the water where the shoe was drifting and took careful steps into the lake while wielding the branch like a fishing pole.

"Go on," Captain Scott instructed.

"But it's cold," Luwann said, a ridiculous plea to make on a hot summer day. He crouched down cautiously, lowered his hands beneath the water surface, and began blindly feeling around, reassuring himself of its shallowness. His lip quivered and he took one step towards the floating sneaker. The water level rose to his kneecaps.

"We'll be here all day waiting for him!" Alex said. In an instant, he ripped open his shirt in Superman fashion, removed his shoes, and ran into the lake. Like a predator stalking a victim, Alex swam in a circle around Luwann, who stopped, becoming a motionless axle to a whirling wake.

With the rest of us, he watched Alex's fluid and determined movements in the water. Alex swam to the shoe, grabbed it, and raised it high. Colonel Cunningham, Captain Scott, my father, and everyone else all applauded the feat.

"It's dirty," Alex said. "But all you have to do is throw it in the washing machine." He tossed the shoe over to Luwann, harder than he needed to. Luwann, dropping the tree branch, caught the shoe and held it against his chest tightly.

"You boys come on and get out of that water before them MP sons of bitches come find you in there," Mr. Lynam said while clapping. "Can't none of you urchins read? The sign says ain't no swimming in this lake. Gone get us thrown out."

"That's some little Cousteau you've got there, Cunningham," my father said to the Colonel. "What else your boy learning in that summer camp?"

"That swimming is nothing," Colonel Cunningham said. "You should see my son handle a knife. Carving things out of wood, you know." He beamed proudly and handed Alex his shirt.

"You're a good swimmer," I told Alex, conceding sheepishly that all his pre-military training had paid off. He nodded a thanks.

"Camp would do your boy good, Scott," Colonel Cunningham said. "It'll work all that timidness right out of him."

"He's not my son, sir," Captain Scott answered. "He's my little brother. It's a program."

I helped Luwann out of the lake and, after the adults walked away—back to their drinking and eating—I helped him put on and tie his wet sneakers.

"Can we be friends?" Luwann asked me.

It took me a long time to answer. "Yeah. We can." His tears dried as I secured the lace knots tight. I told him that the next year, I would take him through the woods and maybe we would find one of those alligators hiding in there. But Captain Scott would bring a different boy to the picnic the following summer. And yet another different boy the summer after that. I would never see my friend Luwann again.

Strivers

(1954)

Florence laughed at her pitiful 17-year-old sister Agnes, dancing there with an imaginary partner, stomping past the old upright piano and second-hand parlor furniture. With her clumsy 4/4 feet incapable of finding rhythm in a waltz played by recorded violins, Agnes pushed away the invisible man and let out an exasperated squeal.

"Here," Florence said. "Let me show you an easy way." Florence stood and tucked a burning cigarette into the corner of her mouth. She had taken up smoking—and wearing Capri pants and traipsing about barefooted—after three and a half semesters at Oberlin. High-schooler Agnes abstained from tobacco and favored floral print dresses and low-heeled pumps, fantasy imitations of the spectators she'd seen advertised in magazines. For waltzing, though, there was no magic in those shoes.

Florence pulled her sister's torso close to her own. Cigarette smoke snaked about easily, causing Agnes's eyes to run. Florence cleared the smoke and began to count out kinetic triplets. "One, two, three, one, two, three. Get that into your head first." Agnes nodded on the ones and emphasized the beat by pounding a fist in a palm. "Good, good," Florence continued. "Now make a box with your feet. It's really simple. Really." She guided Agnes backwards, then to the side, then front, and then to the side again. Agnes wiped a tear from her cheek and looked down to watch her moving feet.

"Beautiful, beautiful," said their mother as she entered with sacks of groceries. She dropped her packages to applaud Agnes's effort.

"How long have you been there, Mother?" Agnes asked.

"Long enough to see that you're almost there, dear—Florence, will you put that cigarette out!"

Florence took one last drag, and, with her thumb and forefinger, bored her last LSMFT into the dirt of a potted plant.

"Your father will be so proud. Let's see it again." Their mother returned the hi-fi's needle to the beginning of the record. Agnes prefaced her box step with a half curtsy. "You're going to be absolutely wonderful, dear," their mother continued. "But you're still a little, I don't know, tight? I'll show you." She reached for Agnes's hips, thinner but less agile than her own. "Graceful, now. Imagine you're atop the clouds," she said, guiding Agnes across the floor. "Don't think about it too much, dear. It should be fun." The two twirled about the room. "Reminds me of dancing with your father the way we used to. He's good, you know."

Florence had never seen her father dance. Not once. He'd bought all those mail-order records—white orchestras playing polite dance music mostly—for relaxing to during his weekends at home. And they made nice companions for their shelfmates, a collection of the *Harvard Classics* which he would leaf through on occasion. But dancing?

"Our father? Dancing?" Florence asked. "I can't imagine."

"No, really," her mother said. "He learned by working in those fancy ballrooms in his younger days. We had an existence before you two came along, you know."

Florence laughed. "Dad *dancing!*"

Winded, the mother stepped away from Agnes, who continued swaying to the lilting string phrases. "You're really getting it. Now, you girls come help me. I've got to get your father's dinner ready. His train comes in at 6:35." The arrival time, always noted with urgency, had not changed in years.

Florence drove her mother and sister to the train station in the family Studebaker. Uncle D.K., who'd personally financed the car, had taught her how to drive like a Northerner, aggressive and focused on the destination, not like a Southerner—lazy and carefree, as if every drive were an after-church recreational activity. Florence could complete the typically thirteen-minute drive from the house to the station in eleven. At 6:32 p.m., she'd parked the car in the station's lot, having already dropped her mother and Agnes at the platform.

Spiting all that was molasses-slow and inefficient about Dixie, the railways ran on time. The whistle blew loudly and precisely at 6:35, boasting of power and punctuality. Even so, Track 2 was terminal, situated in a dead end that made it necessary for a chugging approach to halt and make an excruciating backward crawl, allowing Southern sensibility to win out after all. Holiday travelers, red caps, and others on the platform waited patiently as the cars of the train inched along the tracks and an announcer over the public address speaker briskly rambled down a list of cities the southbound train would pass before reaching its destination in Miami. The engine emitted a steamy sigh and stuttered into a complete stop. With routine swiftness, the red caps hustled to the car doorways and helped passengers with their luggage. Florence huddled with her mother and sister near the wheels of the engine, which, when they were little girls, had seemed as giant as Ferris wheels. The mother always insisted on standing near the front, distanced from any detraining passenger who acted on a need to level a parting indignity towards her husband or any of the other Pullman porters.

"Dad! Dad!" Florence shouted when she saw her father step down from a car in the distance. With his own suitcase and a pink baker's box under his arm, their father performed the last of his duties: helping passengers onto the platform, saying good-bye and probably wishing them all Merry Christmases. After the train's departure gave permission, Florence, Agnes, and their mother rushed to say hello.

Florence hugged her father, who had the appearance of a military general in his dark flat shako hat and white jacket, bright and unblemished except for a minuscule coffee stain on one sleeve. The jacket's collar, still crisp after the thousand-mile journey down the eastern seaboard, cut a pleasant slash across her face.

"How's my college girl?" her father asked, managing to form a weary half-smile ten times more sincere than the full-face beams flashed for the 'drummers,' professional traveling men who feigned wealth and tipped generously. "And my debutante? How's she?"

"You should see how Agnes's dancing is coming along," their mother said. "She's going to be good and ready for Uncle D.K. at the cotillion."

"Oh, yeah?" The father hugged his girls tightly.

"I wish you could be there, Daddy," Agnes said.

"It's a terrible shame they won't give you the day off," Florence added.

"Who travels on Christmas Day, anyway?" Agnes asked.

"Uh, Jews," Florence said in a world-wise way. She'd actually met a few at Oberlin.

"Well, you'd think everyone would be where they need to be by Christmas Day and they could close the trains down," Agnes said. Their father didn't respond, just held out his hands for the car keys and drove home.

The mother cooked a Sunday-worthy meal that Saturday evening, including roasted chicken, the father's favorite. The bird was one of hers from the yard. She knew how to feed them just so, making them plump and juicy, but not so fatty like what they sold at the markets. For dessert, the father had brought New York cheesecake and stacks of magazines left behind by passengers. After dinner, on the parlor floor, Florence and Agnes sprawled out before issues of *Vanity Fair*, *Saturday Evening Post*, and *Ladies Home Journal*.

"No *Harpers*? No *New Yorker*, Daddy? Not even a *Time*?" Florence mock protested as she surveyed the dog-eared periodicals. "Who's riding the train these days?"

"I bring home what I can," their father said. He counted his tip change and placed it neatly across the mantle. Up to eight dollars of it would serve as the upcoming week's emergency fund; the rest would be banked for Agnes's future college tuition.

"I'm just kidding, Daddy, you know that." Florence held up a few of the *Evening Posts*. "These will do."

They usually provided a fine enough read for a story or two. And besides, it was Christmas break for Florence, good to be away from school, classes and pretentious reading lists. Florence snatched a few more magazines from Agnes, who only liked the advertisements anyway.

The mother brought slices of cheesecake and cups of black coffee into the living room for her husband and daughters. "Show your father how good you've gotten, Agnes," she said.

Agnes rose to her feet. "Waltz with me, Daddy."

"No, girl, I don't think so." The father dug into the cheesecake, slightly stale from its journey. It crumbled into large pieces and he savored each one. "Dance with your sister or something. I've been on my feet all day."

"But Mother says you're good. That you really know those ballroom moves."

"Oh, don't listen to your mother. She's the one going around telling the world that it's okay for a porter's daughter to be a debutante in the first place. Your mother has her own unique and strange perspective on things. I'm hardly a dancer of any sort, much less that ballroom prancing."

"I'll dance with you, dear," the mother said, between sips of coffee. "Play for us, Florence."

Agnes and her mother stood together, waiting for Florence to find a waltz to play on the piano.

"Hurry up, Flo," Agnes said. "You should know something by heart."

Florence flipped through one of her old music books and settled on the waltz part of a sonata her piano teacher had forced her to learn years earlier. She smoothed the crinkles on the cream-colored pages, placed the book on the piano, and began. The melody and the fingering came back to her quickly. Looking over her shoulder, she watched her mother and sister dance.

"That's lovely, Agnes," the father said. "You and the Lieutenant will look marvelous at the cotillion together. Just marvelous."

The Lieutenant, Uncle D.K., had gone into the Second World War as an enlisted man, and he liked to tell of a battlefield promotion bestowed by the Army, for some reason, while keeping airplane engines well-greased on the ground in the Philippines. No one ever saw any documents to verify his vault to an officer's rank, but he did have real Lieutenant's bars to show to any doubters. He kept them convenient and shiny and, while at Howard on the GI bill, flashed them at opportune moments to impress coeds. It had worked. Uncle D.K. married his Hettie shortly after graduation. They moved to Chicago, her hometown. She wanted him to go to medical school to become a physician like her own father and brothers were, but Uncle D.K.'s grades were far too sorry for that. Instead, Hettie's father secured an administrator's position for him at the Negro hospital. Uncle D.K. had the personality, if not the smarts, for the job. Excessive handshaking and a knack for making everybody he knew feel like a best friend proved to be useful skills. He made what people in the South called *good* money, but when Florence first visited their matchbox of an apartment on Chicago's Southside, she learned quickly that good money didn't go very far up North.

After finishing the piano piece, Florence turned and

asked, "When's Uncle D.K. getting here, Mother? Is he bringing Aunt Hettie?"

Hettie hated the South and would surely spend an entire visit spying Jim Crow bogeymen and cursing the complacency of docile Southern Negroes.

"Tomorrow, dear," her mother answered. "And of course he's bringing his wife. It's Christmas. No family would spend the holidays apart. Not if they didn't have to."

"Are we done with the recital?" Florence asked. Instead of waiting for an answer, she retreated to her room with an armful of magazines. She loved the illustrations in the *Saturday Evening Post*. She and Agnes had always used them to make collages, saving their creations in oversized scrapbooks given to them one Christmas. Florence began to carefully tear out pictures from the pages of the magazines and arranged them across her bed. One illustration depicted a sly Santa Claus, tiptoeing away from elegantly wrapped presents under a tree. It would be a nice start for a Christmas collage. She needed scissors, the image too good to risk tearing. As Florence stepped from the bed, several of the magazines slipped off the taut spread—tucked in military-style just the way her father had taught them to do. An envelope that escaped from one magazine lay on the floor, address side up, wanting to be discovered. Florence picked up the envelope and read the letter inside:

Ladies Auxiliary, Brotherhood of Sleeping Car Porters, Augusta, Georgia Chapter:

Dear Ladies: The porters below will be working shifts during the holiday. Spouses of those who will be off on the 24th, 25th, and 26th are requested to prepare food care packages for their "adopted" porter!

Let's make the season bright for those who will be working and away from their families this Christmas!

Down the list of porters to be adopted, Florence saw the last names of men she had heard her father talk about often: Johnson, Marshall, and Kenner. There was no Powell. Her father, she decided, would have none of that auxiliary charity. He was too used to her mother's cooking and she would make sure he would be well taken care of with a weeklong holiday picnic. Florence slipped the memo back into one of the magazines, scrapped the collage project, and went to sleep.

Uncle D.K. arrived the next day, just after noon. Whenever he came South, he started the drive in the middle of the night so as to travel in Kentucky, Tennessee, and Georgia during daylight hours. Hettie, who thought of herself as being too young to be called Aunt Hettie by her nieces, charged through the front door first.

"Hi, girls! Where's the, you know, ladies' room?" she asked. Agnes and Florence watched as Hettie wrung her hands and rocked deliriously from side to side. Florence pointed the way. Hettie nodded. "Thanks," she said.

It was a crisp, chilly afternoon, yet Uncle D.K. sweated from carrying Hettie's luggage to the porch. With the brim of his straw fedora, he wiped his brow.

"Hey, hey, how's everybody? All the homefolks doing okay?" His voice boomed and echoed throughout the front parlor. Uncle D.K. kissed his sister and then his nieces, spinning Agnes around like a toy top. "Here's my dancing partner. You ready for your Uncle D.K., baby girl?"

Uncle D.K. looked jowly and much rounder than when

he first started the job in Chicago. It was administrator's girth, Florence determined, achieved by sitting on your ass all day long.

"You're looking good, D.K. Very prosperous," the mother said. "Marriage agrees with you. It's turned you into a real man."

Uncle D.K. shook the father's hand with a jerky exaggerated motion. "Hey there, Porter," he said, doing his best to imitate Jack Benny's Rochester.

"Deek," the father greeted softly, reluctantly using the nickname Uncle D.K. insisted upon. "Have a seat, why don't you?"

"What's the matter with Hettie?" Florence asked. "She headed for the bathroom and barely said hello."

"She had to pee," Uncle D.K. said. His voice lowered. "I told her we could stop at a store, or a church even, since it's Sunday, but you know how she is." Hettie came out of the bathroom. "You all right, honey pie?" Uncle D.K asked. She looked relieved but flush; her normally beige complexion was sickly pink, making her even less attractive than usual. If she weren't his wife, and if her father weren't in charge of the largest colored hospital in the Middle West, the old, younger Uncle D.K. would surely declare that hers was *wasted* yellow.

"Yes, dear," Hettie answered, "I'm okay."

"Well, good. You can go and help Agnes here pick out the dress she wants for the cotillion," Uncle D.K. said. "You know my honey pie here was a deb herself not too long ago." Uncle D.K. pinched his wife's shapely hip.

"Mother has already fixed my dress," Agnes said. "Would you like to see it, Hettie?"

"I'll show you," the mother said. "It's a lovely taffeta gown, store-bought. We got it at Levine's. It needs a little hemming. Come, Agnes, put it on." She led Agnes and Hettie to the dress.

For those remaining in the parlor, awkwardness supplanted the familial pleasantries. Uncle D.K. idly admired the Christmas tree decorations. Florence and her father casually eased back into the Sunday newspaper sections, hiding themselves behind wide-open broadsheets.

"So, what's in the news? Good news? Bad news? No news at all?" an undeterred Uncle D.K. asked.

"Looks like a bit of everything." Florence's voice resonated back to her, sounding cold and mean. She folded the paper down and smiled at her uncle, who held his hat in his lap like a demure lady, fingering the brim ever so gently.

"How come we don't get to see that much of you, Florence?" Uncle D.K. asked. "I thought with you going to school all the way up in Ohio, you'd be visiting us over in Chicago a lot more than you have."

"It's hard to get away during the semester, Uncle D.K. And it takes money, too."

Uncle D.K. reached for his wallet, a large leather billfold he kept in the pocket of his blazer. "If money's the issue we can solve that. Easy." He glanced over the few bills left inside the wallet. "We can send you a check or something, whenever you want to come."

"Put your money away, Deek. There's no call for that. Florence needs to stay put and tend to her studies. She can't be breezing up to Chicago every time she gets the urge."

"I know the book learning is priority number one; I just want Florence to get to know the city better is all," Uncle D.K. said. "There's lots of opportunity for a Negro girl with an A.B.

degree up in Chicago. Much more than down here. Why, we've got dozens of young medical doctors at the hospital just waiting to be snatched up."

"Florence'll do just fine. She can go on to graduate school, come back home and teach at the high school, maybe even the college. Life's not all good for colored people up North," the father said. He eyed Uncle D.K. directly. "I'm up North every week, so that I know."

"It's cold and crowded, Uncle D.K. I don't think I'd like living in Chicago anyway," Florence said.

"Girl, you've got to live there to know that. Colored people get together on their own beach during summertime, you can get around easy, and the nightlife! Clubs, fraternity socials, the Regal Theater. Girls your age take to Chicago like bees to a flower. And if it's teaching you want to do, they *are* schools in Chicago, you know. Talk to my honey pie, will you Florence? She can tell you." Uncle D.K.'s plea seemed desperate. "It'd be nice to have some of *my* family close by." He winked. "Especially my favorite niece."

Florence had seen the lake—not so impressive if you've been to the ocean. She'd also ridden the clanky and crowded L-trains and even smelled the stench of meat-packing plants and crowded apartment flats. But never had she been to the Regal, where Negro stars performed Negro songs, plays, and acts for Negro audiences. "What's the Regal like, Uncle D.K.?" she asked, then girlishly planted her chin in the palm of her hands.

"Oh, the Regal," Uncle D.K. began. He stopped and rose up as Agnes entered the room wearing her cotillion gown and satiny white gloves so long they kissed her elbows. Her mother and Hettie followed behind, corralling pins, needles, and spools of sewing thread. Uncle D.K.'s hat fell to the floor and his eyes blossomed. "Somebody call out to Hollywood, California right now and tell them that Lena Horn is missing and she done showed up right here in Augusta, Georgia." Uncle D.K. took Agnes's hand and marched her up to the Christmas tree. "Ladies and gentlemen, introducing the lovely Agnes Powell, daughter of Mr. and Mrs. Rayburn Powell. She's being presented by her Uncle D.K. of that Great Plains metropolis, Chicago, Illinoise." Agnes laughed and nuzzled her uncle's shoulder.

"You look nice, baby sister," the father said. "Let me go get the camera."

He took pictures of Agnes with Uncle D.K. and her mother.

"Come on, get into the picture, Florence," Uncle D.K. said without breaking his beam. He waved her over.

Florence looked down at herself, her faded cotton blouse, ragged dungarees, tobacco-stained fingers, and bare feet. "I'm not dressed for this scene. Hettie, Dad, you two get in the picture and I'll take it."

"That's enough, anyway," the father said. "I need to save some of the film so you all can take pictures at the cotillion."

"Just one more. Florence and me," Uncle D.K. pleaded.

"No, no, just look at me." Florence tugged on her blouse. "I don't want to be in any pictures looking like this."

Uncle D.K.'s open arms invited Florence over. She huffed, yet reluctantly agreed to pose with him.

The father held the camera to his eye. "Say cheese," he said.

"No," said Uncle D.K. "Say 'Chicago.'"

"Chicagoooo!"

On the last syllable, the father snapped the picture. Florence wondered how the expression on her face would turn out. Bemused puckered lips below fearful widening eyes?

For dinner, for Uncle D.K., the mother made *his* favorite, fried ham with grits and red-eye gravy. He made much over how he couldn't get food like that in Chicago. Even with all those Mississippi Negroes up there, they all seemed to have forgotten how to cook good Mississippi food.

"I never learned how to prepare this kind of food, so my Deek isn't able to get it often," Hettie said. She giggled. "We used to call it slave food."

"We eat it because we like it," the father said to Hettie.

Florence shook her head. Her father had surely had enough of the Lieutenant and his wife. Strivers they were, brown-bloods, haters of their own past, obsessed with light skin, good hair, good times, the first Negro this, and the first Negro that.

"Oh, come on, she didn't mean nothing by it," Uncle D.K. said.

"I've got an early train to catch," the father said before excusing himself from the table.

A prudish questioning scowl grew across Hettie's face. *Who'd be so proud to eat slave food?* it seemed to be saying.

Florence and Agnes woke to Marion the cab driver's rapping at the front door in the middle of the night. They slept in the parlor, having had to give up their beds to Uncle D.K. and Hettie. Their father answered the door and shushed Marion, who was always willing to be available for a 3:00 a.m. fare, even during the holiday season. Sleepy-eyed and quiet, Florence and Agnes watched as their father gathered his jacket from the closet, his suitcase, and a small basket of holiday goodies. The jacket was wrinkled and the coffee stain from the previous run appeared set in, more prominent than before.

"Have a good trip, Daddy," Agnes whispered.

"Go on back to bed," the father said. He blew kisses to his daughters.

"I can take you to the station, Daddy," Florence said.

"No, no, Marion's here," he said.

Marion grabbed the picnic basket. "Boss, your wife sure set you up good for the holidays," he said after peeking inside.

"Yeah. I'll be gone the whole week," the father said.

"How far your run is this week: Washington? Philadelphia? New York? Boston?"

The front door closed on Marion's gushing on about how he too wanted to be a porter, see the country, earn good money, and wear such a sporting white uniform jacket.

"Daddy didn't have his hat," Agnes said absently. She yawned and returned to her sleep.

Florence imagined some supervisor with an evil drawl reprimanding her father for leaving it behind. She could see a wagging finger before her father's bowed head. Their mother's efforts to shield Florence and Agnes from such confrontations seemed only to help magnify their perceived severity, and the impact they must have had on their father. Florence got up, found the hat and the Studebaker keys, and headed for the station.

Six blocks away, she heard the train's whistle. It echoed calmly throughout the empty downtown streets. The Studebaker revved loudly as Florence sped up. Nearing the station, she could see the cars of the train parked on Track 2. Sleeping heads rested against the frosted windows inside the train and shadows moved through the aisles. They were still boarding. She reached for her father's porter hat, got out of the car, and ran barefoot across cold concrete towards the track platform. Seconds later, the whistle blew again, in forceful whole notes, and the train began to slowly chug away.

"Shit," Florence whispered. "Shit!" The passing cars revealed a mounted clock declaring the time to be 3:20 and a lone figure sitting on a bench at the end of the platform. She recognized her mother's picnic basket first, then as she got closer, Florence saw her father's face. His eyes met hers, then darted down towards the hat.

"What are you doing here?" he asked, his eyes still focused on the hat.

"I thought you might need this. I didn't know what they might do to you, Daddy. I'm sorry I was late. I drove as fast as I could."

"You came in your bare feet? Good Lord! Cold as it is?"

"I didn't want you to get in trouble. Those bastards didn't let you make the run because you didn't have it?" Florence took a seat next to her father. "Don't they have extra ones? And it's not like you've got to have it on to do your job. Those bastards."

"Girl, you see..." her father began. He reached out for one of Florence's hands, rubbing it for warmth, perhaps to soothe her. "I wasn't really scheduled to make a run this week."

Florence pulled her hand back and gripped the cap tightly. "Then why did you say so? Why are you here?"

"Now, don't go getting angry with me. I just didn't want to be a part of it all. Not this thing."

"What *thing*? Christmas with your family after spending weeks and weeks on the railroad? Oh, the agony."

"Not Christmas. Agnes's cotillion. That's her domain— your mother, I mean. I didn't want her to miss out on it. She loves it so. Stubborn you wouldn't participate, now Agnes gives her a last chance. But I can't mix with those people, so instead of making an issue…"

"You choose to run away? What are you afraid of, Daddy? You've seen the whole country, read all those damned *Harvard Classics*. What have they got on you?"

As her father searched for an answer in the palms of his open hands, a patrolman locked and exited the station. He cheerily whistled what sounded like a Christmas carol.

"You missed your train, porter?" the patrolman asked.

"No. No, sir."

"You all will need to get going. It's mighty cold out here. Station's closed."

"I'm just waiting for my ride. It'll be here directly."

"And you?"

"This is my father. I'm with him."

"That not your automobile over there?" the patrolman asked, nodding towards the Studebaker.

"You better get on home, Florence," the father said.

"It broke down. We're waiting for a lift."

"Okay—but your ride better get here soon. I can't leave you two just sitting here." The patrolman picked up his whistling again, locking in the melody of *White Christmas*, and walked away.

"Florence, I'd like you to go home. And let's keep this to ourselves. It's best."

"Where are you going to be for four whole days? Who's picking you up? A lady?" Florence feared the answer.

"I'm still your father. But if you must know, one of the young porters is stopping by. He lives with his family across the river, out in the country, in South Carolina."

"You're staying the whole week?"

"That's the plan. You know, he's around your age. Maybe you should stay and meet him."

"Why didn't you just go over to his place tonight?"

"Oh, you know Marion. He's got a big mouth."

Florence kissed her father on the forehead and placed the cap in his lap. He looked so weary, cold, and alone on the bench. She kissed him again. "Don't worry, Daddy," she said. "I won't say anything."

The Interview

Before entering the building at 2600 Park Springs Drive, Spartanburg, South Carolina, I lowered a brand new leather bag to the ground, swabbed droplets of sweat across my forehead, looked skyward, and caught glimpses of the sun. The ruthless hellfire dared me, and all its other hapless victims, to go ahead, just try to cool off. I squinted and discovered deep inside the sun's core the colors of my very first Career Day.

Those two words, zealously scrawled in a fat script emblazoned by reddish-orange Magic Marker ink, overflowed the borders of April 17 on the oversized calendar hanging in my first grade classroom, over fifteen years earlier. Our teacher, Mrs. Walters, had scheduled the celebration in a month void of any holidays to ease the spring blues seeping into us, a usually electrified assortment of six-year-olds from solid middle- to upper-middle-class homes who had been waiting for the summer itinerary of overnight camps, Rehoboth or Outer Banks beach trips, and academic enrichment programs at the University of Maryland. As Career Day approached, it became apparent that participating in what would become an annual ritual in our elementary school required providing one of the most important answers of our lives.

Mrs. Walters sternly warned just that. She boosted our very limited understanding of what people could do and become in life by posing a multiple-choice question, strategically and artistically applying the answers on the cinder block wall in the form of brightly colored construction paper cutouts. There was a policeman, a fireman, a train engineer, a doctor, a judge, a teacher, a nurse, a businessman, and a spiritual leader denoted with an angelic aural overhead and hands folded in nondenominational prayer. The images encircled the calendar, lined the doorway, and cluttered the typically empty space above the twenty-five prongs where we hung our coats. Those smiling cartoon characters, existing in a happy two-dimensional fantasy world where earning paychecks made people spry and ruddy, seemed all too eager to put on their occupational uniforms, announce themselves to the world, and celebrate that they had *become* what was ordained for them to *become*.

Mrs. Walters, a spirited Seven Sister *sistah* infused with both a post-modern independent streak and pre Civil Rights-era sensibilities, tried to inspire our choices with the words of community heroes, the generic and non-race-specific name bestowed upon civil and human rights leaders at our school, an austere Friends institution shrouded by million-dollar homes and a 19th Century Quaker idealism we'd formally learn by 7th grade. These pellets of inspiration constantly knocked about in our heads like a noise in a defective car, and they were to be recited upon request:

If I can conceive it and believe it, I can achieve it...

Jesse said that, and everybody knows that.

THE INTERVIEW

It is not enough to understand, or to see clearly. The future will be shaped in the arena of human activity, by those willing to commit their minds and their bodies to the task...

Bobby Kennedy said that. They had to dig for that one. Most of us surely had no idea what it meant, and we often scrambled to piece together the words in their correct order when called upon to recite the line from memory.

I am somebody. It's not my aptitude, but my attitude that will determine my altitude...

More Jesse.

He had a dream...

that one day I could dress up as anything I wanted to... on Career Day.

(No clarification needed about the "he" in question. They had posters all over school by the first week of January to remind us).

So, with the clearest of visions, I conceived myself as and committed myself to becoming the cartoon man wearing the suit. The one in gray pinstripes, toting a briefcase and smiling slyly—it seemed—towards the real-life generic-branded clock ticking in the rear of the room. A happy clock-watcher he was. That's who I wanted to be. It'd be easy enough to wear my Easter clothes and call it a Career Day.

Mrs. Walters thought my choice bold, since others reached for jobs and career titles with obvious duties and skill requirements identifiable to a six-year-old. Others proclaimed they would turn out to be what their parents had become, a hodgepodge of the traditional professionals endemic to a Washington, D.C. elite that produced nothing tangible, just tedious policies, think-tank tomes, windy academic theories, unenforceable laws and regulations bound in volumes upon volumes of GPO printed books destined, eventually, for a landfill.

Mrs. Walters made mention of how much of a little man I looked in my own gray pinstriped short set and red Charles Shultz-inspired necktie, paraded me around and told me in order to get the most out of my attire, I needed to have a stiff back and upright shoulders. With a balled fist positioned against my lower spine, she cocked me upwards to demonstrate the appropriate posture for a Man in A Suit, a Brooks Brothers superhero with real-life powers beyond Superman and Batman combined. She led me down the center aisle in the classroom, the catwalk for our little fashion show. Then she asked me why. Why did I want to become the man in the suit?

I turned towards her. My eyes veered upward and locked on the savory light green circles that dabbed some color into her pale visage. I stammered. "Be-be-be-cause they make the most money of them all."

It was pure conjecture and quite the wrong thing to be saying at a school started by Quakers and run by their modern-age ideological descendants who drove second-hand Volvos, ordered clothes from L.L. Bean and, following the leads of their dual-income and practical-minded friends, vacationed economically in beachside timeshares. And really, the truth was that I had no idea how much money men who wore suits earned or where their earnings stood on America's socio-economic ladders. I had no points of reference. My father spent his days in white doctor's coats; my mother trotted out the house three days a week to teach future teachers in her flower print dresses and open-toed high-heeled shoes or off-white blouses, monochrome skirts, and bookish, sensible—very sensible—black pumps.

A few kids in the class laughed at my answer. I tried to reassemble it into something that would find the approval of my teacher and my peers.

"Mrs. Walters, I want to be a man in a suit because they are very important people."

"That's great, Samuel," she said. "It's nice to be important, but what, class?"

In unison, my classmates responded, "It's important to be nice!" Some wagged their fingers at me as they shouted, reminding me of the violation of a learned Quaker ethos. Others wondered aloud whether their career choices were *nice* or *important.* I cried and bolted from Mrs. Walters's room, determined to enjoy a pressure-free adolescence without thinking about what my adult job would be for years and years to come.

I wouldn't have to. I never thought I'd have a job anyway. Fate had assumed that I, Samuel Rogers Jenkins, III, would just *become* something.

Prosecutor.

Astronaut.

Biomedical engineer.

Such were the pre-teen responses I gave to that ritualistic adult query, *What do you want to be when you grow up?*

"How nice," the questioner would say, before caressing the bushy black curls sprouting atop my head and marveling at the changed times. That a little black boy growing up in the formerly officially segregated South that was Washington, D.C. could hold and possibly realize such lofty career aspirations was the wondrous result of—depending on the questioner's politics—the continual and determined underground efforts of black liberationists, the civil rights movement, or the inherent goodness of the American dream. I'd be urged to pay homage to those who had variously paved ways, spilled blood, and risked livelihoods so I could one day believe in the reality of equal opportunity. When teen angst and rebellion settled in, I'd gotten smart-lucky with my answers.

Night manager at Burger King.

Maintenance engineer at a print shop.

Sports information director for an all-girls college.

Assistant garbage collector.

I'd offer such replies, knowingly concealing an assumption I knew to be true: I'd become a doctor. A physician. The medical doctor. Not one of the fuddy-duddies who "teach" at colleges and have messy dreadlocked hair.

My father was one, and his brother was one; they seemed content, and made shiploads of money. At least cousins, friends, and neighbors implied that—sneered it even. I never saw much of this legendary green which had apparently settled somewhere in a chasm between my father's tight ways and his perpetual life lessons on independence. So, at age sixteen, over a Sunday dinner of roast beef, green beans almandine, red-skinned mashed potatoes, and sour cream pound cake, I announced to my parents that I was to become a physician, a sports medicine specialist so as to intertwine my passion for sports with my eagerness to become someone who could afford a new Benz every six years.

"That's a fine idea," my mother said, chewing a mouthful of her always-good cooking, not looking up from her dinner plate. "Good healthcare is going to be so important if we want to continue to progress as a people. Bad nutrition, high blood pressure, cholesterol, cancer, four hundred years of baggage causing all kinds of mental issues—it's all killing us. You'd be making a measurable contribution to your community."

My father reached across his station at the head of the dining room table and rubbed my nape. Between smacking on potatoes—his mouth rotating and rumbling like an overused laundry mat dryer—he told me that I'd have to study hard and get good MCAT scores. He pondered the possibility of my inheriting his practice and office space at Georgia Avenue and Gallatin, NW, a stuffy former residence with tattered carpeting and a thousand and one paint jobs. I'm pretty sure it wasn't a joke, though he laughed whenever he repeated this, which was often after that day. His eyes would float off to some distant vision of me poring over a sickly Medicaid patient in one of his examination rooms. I'd crinkle my nose in response. His dilapidated, seedy office space needed to be decontaminated and demolished, not inherited.

With good grades and stratospheric-for-D.C.-students SATs, I entered college predicting that intellectual stimulation and the sheer aura of ivy-covered ancient buildings would transform my high school A's into respectable college B's. And I would surely ace whatever the hell Organic Chemistry was, the course my cock-eyed freshmen advisor said separated the pre-meds from the *pretend*-meds.

"Racist joker," I balked. My racial consciousness and inner Huey Newton, unearthed and then re-buried all within the nine-month window of my freshman year, had me dismissing the advisor as just the first in a conspiratorial line of white men attempting to steer me away from my destiny. However, I never made it to organic chemistry to prove him wrong. A senior econ major assigned as my mentor by the university's African-American Student Affairs department schooled me on the best route to the easy dollar: business.

"Finance, my brother," he said, close in and confidential-like, punctuating the dropped knowledge with a succession of fist pats to the chest. The mentor said he knew more miserable MDs; overworked resident physicians working for slave wages and saddled with debt while young, working too many hours in their middle ages, and just too old when they finally had time to enjoy their banked wealth. I took his advice all the way to registration and signed up for *Introduction to Accounting*, announced myself as a business and economics major, and from then on, told anyone who asked that I was to become a businessman.

My parents held three visions of a *Businessman*. There were the respectable entrepreneurs *in business*; the original black capitalists, eager sons and grandsons of slaves who, armed with unbounded optimism and Washingtonian (Booker T., not George) initiative, honorably served the black communities of contentedly segregated America. They opened and operated barber and beauty shops, funeral homes, grocery and specialty stores, movie theatres, and sit-down restaurants. They sold burial insurance policies for pennies, and teased the senses of a new black middle class with touchable things like furniture, flooring, lampshades, and carpets; commodities you could smell, like kerosene and vanilla-scented lye soap; goods you could taste, like buttery yeast biscuits and peppered stew meat. All this commerce occurred in comfortable, modest neighborhoods that would later see riots, decay, renewal, and gentrification. They'd pass on their entrepreneurial know-how to their children, who would grow the businesses and use their profits as stepping stones to even more profitable ventures, like politics and allowing their money to make them money, just like rich white people do.

But then, there were also the hustlers who *did business,* on street corners, in the beauty salons and barbershops, at makeshift flea markets, and in the back rooms of residences in the same neighborhood. Sometimes legally, but mostly not, *they* sold hubcaps, dresses "imported" from Paris by way of family connections in Brooklyn, used appliances, shrink-wrapped meat with scratched-out price stickers and unknown origins. Whatever the market of the moment demanded, they always found ways to produce the supply.

The third group, in my parents' world view, were the inheritors of the revolution, the civil rights babies who, in their starched white collars, polyester Sears suits and cat-eye glasses, *entered business* through the doorways of companies with pedigreed brands and headquartered in somebody's Oz-like Emerald City. The black weekly newspapers would announce their appointments on the social page, and churches would pray them off to futuristic skyscrapers in faraway downtowns and low-lying office parks in sprawling suburbs. What they actually did in those buildings, and the battles fought within, remained a mystery to most back home or back in the neighborhood. It was this third type of businessman my parents agreed would be okay to become.

Four years later, with a transcript littered with moderately respectable grades, I still wasn't exactly sure what kind I wanted to be. Summer internships at major corporations did little to help the cause. And while my classmates had Wall Street brokerage firms, management consulting positions, and ancient banks in their lines of sight, the only in-person interview I could score was for an account management position with an industrial tool manufacturer in Spartanburg, South Carolina. No one wants to become an account manager. It sounded like a *job*. But by April of my senior year, reality hit: I wasn't becoming anything, and I didn't have a prospect to even lie about to my parents or myself. The interview in Spartanburg I secured on my own, and got it because of my own initiative. I felt proud of that, like one feels about a hard-earned B.

So, with the morning Carolina sun giving my forehead a beat-down, I took a deep breath and walked into the building, the capstone of an office park nestled between symbols of the *new* New South: a freshly paved multi-lane interstate highway and a strip shopping center containing a Target on steroids, a themed family restaurant, a travel agency promoting Caribbean destinations in its front windows, and a small commercial zoo masquerading as a chain pet store.

As instructed, I took the elevator to the fifth floor, the main administrative offices of TGM, Ltd., the largest industrial tool manufacturer and distributor east of the Mississippi, South of the Mason-Dixon, and north of Tallahassee, Florida. The receptionist was blonde and milky white, just as my friend and college classmate Margaret said they all would be. She didn't just say that, she *warned* it as a last-ditch effort to get me to forget the trip, the interview, and the little company where even the lowest of the lowest employees—like the receptionist—would look nothing like me. As I entered the TGM office, I remembered Margaret's parting question, which she slipped in after polite Euro-chic cheek kisses that morning at the airport: "Why do *you* think they're paying your way to go down there?" I could answer only with a kiss of my own.

"Can I help you?" the receptionist asked.

Her singing voice erased a nice memory of Margaret's soft lips and concerned eyes. The receptionist couldn't have been more than 18 or 19 years old. A chunky class ring hung from her necklace and she kept yanking the loop slightly as if it were an annoyance, but too dear to remove.

"Yes, I'm here for the interview. Mr. Logan is the one I'm looking for," I said in a rhythmic cadence and my best inflected articulate Negro voice.

"Oh, he's expecting you." She punctuated the "you" and stretched it out all the way until it became a smelly female sheep: "eeeyeeew."

"Mr. Logan, he's here," she said into the telephone, softly while smiling at me, as if protecting some devilish secret. She hung up. "He'll be with you. You'll have a Coke or something to drink?"

"No, I'm okay."

The smile on her face turned into a lippy half-frown. It was the hardened cracker-ish look—the same slivery eyes I'd seen in pictures of old Southern sheriffs or in Hollywood movies with KKK characters unveiling themselves. The look triggered a shiver within me, until I reminded myself that this was just a surly Spartanburg teenager, pissed at the world in general, not me specifically.

"Suit yourself." The receptionist adjusted her computer monitor to get a better view of the aquarium screen saver bubbling on it. She then picked up a romance novel, rested it on her ample gut, and began to read—or at least move her eyes over the page. I sat, stared out a nearby window, and eyed a sprawling new industrial plant in the distance. Parts of its massive exterior were literally in some kind of building shrink-wrap. I could see that the grass in the surrounding expanse had been freshly planted. The sterile newness of the view and the hum of traffic coming from the nearby interstate put me in a hypnotic trance as I tried to trace the specific steps that led me to this spot.

The journey seemed so random. I'd first read about TGM, Ltd. in an in-flight magazine during a spring break trip to Cancun that I battled my parents to go on in the first place. The article, a puff piece that would have been equally at home in a Spartanburg Chamber of Commerce newsletter, featured up-and-coming private companies in the Carolinas. The blurb about TGM came from an analyst who said this company was "one to watch" because of "cutting-edge" approaches to distribution and a "seasoned management team." From there, several months later, it became a class project for *Marketing 360*—pick a company, any company, predict the outlook for it within its industry, and tell why. The semester would be long gone before my lame analysis of TGM could be proven wrong. I said it'd move into a top twenty position in its market because the CEO was a knowledgeable go-getter and he had taken a prestigious management course in France. But as a private company, TGM lacked the capital that its top competitors had, one of whom would steal TGM's cutting-edge approach to distribution. That being so, TGM wouldn't crack the top ten for years to come. "B" the professor gave me, as they are wont to do, for work that's reasonably logical, but really isn't that good. For sixteen weeks, I studied the company's Website, press releases, and every brochure they had issued. I knew every officer's name, where they had gone to school, who they married, who they divorced and, in the case of the CEO, I even knew his favorite vacation spot: Disneyland. In a survey published in *Today's Executive*, the TGM CEO said he liked Disney's parks because they are the one domestic destination that put smiles on the faces of his kids, and because something felt so damned right about spending money with one of the best maintained brands in the world. The article listed all the things the CEO said he liked about the Disney brand: Uncompromising quality. Strategic boldness. An ultimate exemplification of the best of America's core values.

After the first semester of senior year ended, and on-campus job interviews produced only a stack of "thanks but no thanks" responses, I emailed a résumé to TGM, regurgitating in the cover letter bits and pieces from my class project. I heard back from a "Christa in HR" within two weeks. I did a phone interview with her, a motherly woman who spent half the conversation asking me about growing up in the corrupt sewer of Washington, D.C. She said *they* liked my résumé, how much I knew about them, and the go-getter attitude that came across over the phone. They wanted to see me in person to sniff out if we were a good fit. That's the way she said they put it: a good fit. I imagined myself lodged in the fingertips of an anxious old-time gamer hovering a puzzle piece over a half-finished picture puzzle, spying the open spaces and looking for the perfect connection; the perfect fit.

With the reality of seeing and smelling the place, a nauseous feeling engulfed my stomach. My shoulders tensed, my hands sweated. I wished that I had taken up the receptionist on her offer for a Coke. Perhaps it would have calmed my nerves. I flashed a kindly smile as I prepared to ask for something to drink. A booming baritone disrupted my state of hesitancy.

"Sorry to keep you waiting, son," Logan said as he entered the reception area. I felt and took in the presence of this man. He stood straight up tall—6' 4" maybe—and had a blocky robotic face that didn't quite match his doughy offensive lineman's frame. "Delores here didn't offer you anything?"

I stood to shake his hand, remembering to do so firmly, resolutely. I worried that he'd rightfully interpret my clamminess as anxiety.

"I tried," Delores the receptionist said. "He didn't want anything."

"Yes, I'm fine, Mr. Logan," I said. "It's a pleasure to finally meet you."

I followed behind Logan, down a hallway done up in TGM's corporate colors—bright red, green, and ocean blue. The offices looked like the set of a children's TV show, and at each desk in every office, grown-up kids yakked it up on phones or stared blankly at glowing computer screens. Logan's office turned out to be a corner one, the second one we had passed on our walk.

"Have a seat, son," he said.

I sat in a green chair, one of three opposite Logan's desk. A matching metal shelf loomed behind him. There were a few books on the shelf—one on success written by a championship-winning college football coach—lots of mementos, and these curious transparent plastic cubes encasing tiny little booklets.

"Done deals," said Logan, nodding slowly.

"Huh? Sir?"

"Each one of those represents done deals." He pointed, methodically, to each of the cubes. "At TGM, we're about partnering, not about selling." It was a quote I'd seen in a TGM brochure on its Website. I was going to say so, but thought it better not to.

"Yeah, I have a professor who'd been with Coke who says the same thing," I said. I was lying; my professor had said no such thing. But I wanted him to think that I thought what he said was something meaningful and impressive. If a business academic said it too, it must be so.

"Oh, I don't have much faith in those university and b-school boys," Logan said. "The ones I've met can't walk and chew gum at the same time. But if this fellow worked at Coke then he can't be all bad." Logan looked reflectively at the shelf of done deals. "Now there's a company. Them boys over in Atlanta make damned 'colored flavored water,' and it's the best-known brand name in the world. Folk in the jungles of Timbuktu even know Coca-Cola, and just by the shape of the bottle, which they don't even use that much anymore. I read that somewhere. Or was it something I saw while flipping past PBS?" Logan's eyes shifted from the shelf and then to my face. "Course, we aren't here to talk about Co-Cola. So, tell me son, why TGM?"

"I was doing this report for a class," I began, nervously. Logan had already shown his disdain for academics; he was sure to not be impressed by my pathetic class project. "It started really with this article I read about top private companies in the South."

"You mean this one?" Logan surreptitiously retrieved a magazine from his desk drawer and opened it to a page marked with a paper clip. "See my picture, did you?" Logan pointed to his face in a photo of TGM executives. He was in the back. All except his face was hidden.

"Yes, sir, I did."

"So we got you to come all the way done here to Spartanburg on account of a magazine article? If you get hired and turn out to be a good salesman then I guess the bribe to the magazine publisher was worth it." Logan laughed again.

I went on, telling him about my class project, my analysis of TGM, and about my summer internships at IBM and Coors. I opened my brown leather portfolio and one by one spread across his desk my résumé and three letters of recommendations from professors who barely knew me. I told him of my eagerness to learn and do business at a place that produces real things for real people. Stocks, securities, financial "instruments"? That was for bluebloods, golden boys. Wall Street wannabes. Technology, software, and computers? That was for geeks. I wanted to get my hands dirty and know what it was like to sell things that help working people work, businesses build, and machines to operate.

Logan told me of the joyous feelings he got by working for a place that does help put Americans to work. He told me how, as long as Americans build, they will need tools to do it. That market promised a bright future, and TGM had the marathon runner's legs to be in the race for the long haul. I answered that he spoke of exactly what I wanted: a place in it for the long haul.

"Well, that's all good to know," Logan said after our exchange of patriotic pleasantries and my well-rehearsed interview spiel. "But I just got three more questions for you son."

"Okay."

"Then I'll turn you over to Lou and the boys to see what they think. You ready?" He looked at me hard, like a pitcher waiting for a signal from his catcher. He flashed the fastball sign.

"Yes," I answered.

The university's placement center emailed all seniors a handbook during the first week of classes. In between sections on "dressing for success" and "targeting your job search," they included a tip sheet on the top twenty interview questions. Every interviewer surely would rattle off three or four, the sheet proclaimed, and almost all asked, "Where do you see yourself in five years?" But Logan's three questions were nowhere on that list, at least as I was remembering it sitting there in his office, feeling small in the little green chair across from a giant of a man with a shelf full of done deals.

He asked, in this order exactly:

"If I hire you, will you always work as hard as you can for me?"

"If your answer is yes, do I have your word on it?"

"Will TGM be your number one priority?"

"Answer truthfully now," Logan went on. "Smart young fellow like you got no reason to lie."

I thought for several seconds. I then thought that thinking about it probably wasn't a good idea. Logan didn't want thoughtful schoolboy answers. He wanted me to show him I had instincts. But I didn't want to sound glib, like a fast talker. The Coke professor reminded us that Southerners hate fast-talking Northerners who crowd their words to sound smart or conceal true motives.

"Yes, yes, and no, probably number two," I said.

Logan took a second to sync my answers with his questions. "That's good, son. I like honesty. You can't partner with anybody if they aren't being honest. Number two, heh? I'm giving you the thumbs-up this go round," he said. "Course, what I think don't mean much. At TGM, we play team ball." Logan tapped his speakerphone and dialed a number.

A voice answered in two rhythmic triplets: "Tee Gee Emm, this is Lou."

"Lou, it's Logan. We're ready for you."

"Okay," the voice said.

Logan led me through a maze of cubicles, each cluttered with notebooks, papers, Coke cans, obnoxious orange sports posters, and other paraphernalia from nearby Clemson University—tiger paws, tiger statues, miniature orange helmets and such. When we got to Lou's cube, he was standing, talking on a headset and gesturing a lot with his hands. Lou continued his phone conversation.

"Well, that's what we're here for, John… If I can't make it happen for you, then I'm not doing my job, John… What's it going to take?"

Logan beamed. Lou hung up the phone. "Son of a bitch!" Lou shouted. "Trying to play me! Play *me*! Man, that shit works my nerve." He and Logan high-fived awkwardly, white-boy style, carefully making sure the palms of their hands met and the contact was low-impact. Lou sighed and ripped his headset off.

"Lou here is the best," Logan said. He introduced us. We shook hands.

"I'm second best, really. Hi ya doing? It can get crazy here, but it's a great place to work. Gives me a real buzz. Industrial tools?" Lou's voice slipped up to an excited soprano. "Who the hell knew?"

"Well, I'm leaving you two boys alone. We'll talk later, Lou," Logan said. He patted Lou on the back twice.

"Sure thing," Lou answered. His phone rang. "Damn, I need to get that. You want to wait over in the conference room?"

Lou put his headset back on and went to work. From the conference room, I watched as he rolled up the sleeves of his white oxford shirt. Again, he paced and gestured as he talked. For several minutes, he carried on this way, pointing, weaving, and bobbing as if the person on the other end were the heavyweight champion battling right there in the cubicle with him. He picked up a hand-sized toy football and cocked his arm back as if to throw passes, short darts to flankers cutting across the middle. The phone call ended and Lou spiked the ball on his desk. It bounced and fell to the floor.

"I tell you," he said as he entered the conference room. "Everybody's trying to play me for a fool today. Waste my time. Time is money, don't they know?" He sat across the table from me and propped his scuffed-up burgundy penny loafers on the cushioned seat of a new-looking office chair. "So, you go by Sam? Sammy?"

"Samuel's fine."

"Okay, Samuel, what'd you think of Logan? He's a killer huh?"

"I guess you could say that's why I wanted to interview here," I said.

"Yeah, we took one look at that résumé of yours and knew you had some killer experience. We could use some of that. Got that new car plant in town. We've been trying to nail down a whopper of an account over there. Big boys like that eat up the kind of big-time experience you got. Having you on board would be good for the team."

During my summer at IBM, I replaced the vacationing mailroom workers and did data entry, and at Coors I sat in on a bunch of diversity seminars and drank lots of half-priced beer.

"How's the team here?" I asked, quickly wanting to change the subject.

"Aw, man, working here, it's killer," Lou said. "I mean, we're competitive and all, but these guys are all friends in the office and pretty much outside too." Lou waved his hand over the maze of cubicles like an evangelist with healing powers. "We're going out tonight if you're interested. Rich is getting married next week and we're taking him out. Just us boys. No girlfriends or wives. You should come. Rich manages my group, Team Tiger. He's a good person to get to know."

I laughed. "Oh, I don't know if it would make too good of an impression—the interviewee going out before the decision is made."

"Oh, Sam—I mean Samuel—Logan likes you. I can tell."

"Yeah, how's that?" I asked.

"He gave me the signal."

"The signal?"

Lou reached over and patted my back twice. "The signal."

"So, where is this pre-wedding soirée for Rich going to be?" I asked. I felt a goofy grin creep up the sides of my cheeks.

"Where you staying, at the Jennifer Hotel downtown, right?"

"Yeah, that's right."

"Perfect. It's going to be right down the street, at this dive tit bar called Minks. We'll see you around 7:00 p.m.?"

"I suppose. Is this it?"

"Unless you got any questions or anything that can't wait until tonight, then yeah, that's it," Lou said. "I've got to get back to work anyway. My numbers have been in the crapper this month, man." Lou gave himself a Bronx cheer and positioned his headset back on his head, just as a quarterback would adjust his helmet before getting back into the game.

I headed for the hotel and tried napping in my suit, carefully sleeping on my back, stiffly as in a coffin. I changed into jeans before going out.

In the hotel lobby, I lingered around the front desk for a bit, searching for a comfortable stance. The Jennifer Hotel's lobby was not exactly a hotbed of activity, yet the desk clerk ignored me as she hastily rambled through some papers.

Words spilled from my mouth. "Excuse me, can you give me directions to a place called Minks, or something like that? I'm supposed to meet some people there tonight."

"Minks. You sure that's the place you want to go?" The clerk never looked up.

"That's what they told me. The people who invited me there," I clarified for her.

"It's not in the best part of town, you know." Her tone was motherly. She looked at me, then pointed out the door of the hotel. "Just walk down in that direction for, I don't know, eight or so blocks. You'll know it when you come to it."

It was close to 7:00 p.m. and the town's sidewalks were empty until I reached Minks, fronted by a neon sign depicting two kissing animals. The wooden front door of the place swung open several times as I approached. Each time the door opened, pulsating electro-beats from a wretchedly bad sound system grew louder.

"I.D.?" a scruffy bouncer at the door asked. I showed him my driver's license and university I.D. card; he barely glanced at them and waved me in.

Purple velvet decorated most of Minks—or at least the spotlights made everything look purple. Even the bodies of the mostly naked women gyrating on a small runway stage were bathed in soft violet hues. I navigated the musty and claustrophobic interior, winding around a few bolted-down, theatre-style seats that faced a stage. I saw TGM Lou at a table near the front with three others, all in wrinkled white Oxford shirts and loosened striped ties. The performing stripper wiggled in front of the TGM foursome, and Lou made some remark that caused the woman to giggle and interrupt her choreography. She regained her demeanor and glided to the opposite side of the stage. Lou rose as I approached. He smelled of beer they must have drunk before they got to Minks. Typical of Southern logic—I learned—strip clubs in the city weren't allowed to serve beer if the place showed nipples. Alcohol mixed with the site of a bare erect pink nipple would spawn revelry, rape, and mayhem. However, if the strippers wore pasties, it was a non-issue and customers were able to drink up. At Minks, they showed nipples.

Lou hugged me in b-boy fashion, then introduced me to the team. Membership must have required having a one-syllable name. "Chuck, Stein, Rich, this here is Sam," Lou said. "He's coming on board."

I shook their hands and corrected my name. They didn't pay attention to that; they all called me Sam for the rest of the night. I didn't even try to explain that I had no offer and, even if I did, I wasn't sure if I'd take the job.

Rich, the team boss and the one who was getting married, initiated the first bit of conversation with me. Taller and older than the others, he wore a Marine buzz cut and the expressionless face of an underwear model. "What you make of Logan?" Rich asked.

"I like him," I said.

A new stripper began to perform. A skinny blonde, her tremendous and obviously augmented breasts drooped like half-filled water balloons nailed to a pole. She must have been a favorite of the regulars, including the TGM foursome. They cheered her and mockingly pleaded for some special trick involving a water glass. Rich punched me on the shoulder, friendly-like, before commenting that the move was "patented" and "technically illegal" according to some secret city ordinance.

"You'll be telling everybody back at school about this one," Lou added. The pleas went unheeded. The erotic dancer refused to perform her trick. Her eyes passed mine several times during her dance and darted away each time. Seeing my unfamiliar face in the place, I feared she must have thought I was an undercover cop or something, ready to shut the place down should any illegal acts be conducted. I felt bad. Lou and the others were ready to tip her generously from the wads of skuzzy dollar bills that filled their hands. From the look in her eyes, she really wanted (or needed) the money.

"I'm sorry you missed the trick," Lou said after the dancer finished. "It's really something special." He hinted what the trick was with a twisting of his hip followed by a deep knee bend. "But you'll get your chance when you move down here. We do this at least once a month."

"Once a month?" My voice lilted; the sound of incredulity rose above the music.

"Yeah. That don't make us pervs or anything in your book, do it, Sam?"

"No," I answered. Lou scanned me up and down as if to re-size me up. As if he'd mis-pegged me in the office. But he was too drunk to care. Lou's attention turned back to the stage as another dancer was set to begin her gyrations. From the bottom of his diaphragm, he let loose a big whoop and called out a name. I chuckled nervously at it all for no apparent reason.

"We like him too," Rich said, interrupting my laughter.

"Huh?" I asked.

"Logan. We like him too." Rich said again. "For me, he's like a father figure of sorts." His eyes focused on the dancer. The club announcer called her Special K.

"One helping is never enough!" a deep, black-sounding voice shouted over the speakers. "Eat Special K every morning, noon, and night, and you'll feel all right!"

THE INTERVIEW

Special K, a redhead with all-natural body parts and the figure of a young woman who'd been through some shit in life, didn't garner the same enthusiastic response as the first dancer did, but the crowd approved of her general charisma and exaggerated pole humping. She shimmied her flat ass over to Rich. He tipped her, slipping a crisp five-dollar bill inside a white lace garter that needed the acquaintance of a bottle of bleach.

"See that girl there?" Rich nodded towards the stripper doing her thing. "Kristen's her real name. We grew up together right around the corner from here. In the projects." Images of fenced-in high-rise towers, cinderblock walls, and the smell of ammonia entered my mind. And then I remembered that we were in the South. Rich's projects were probably almost-quaint garden apartments or spacious family duplexes fronting lawns. "Logan gave me a chance," Rich said. "I was in the Army, did a couple of college-boy years at USC Upstate, and was drifting around from sales job to sales job—I sold everything from washing machines to commercial time at a TV station—until I met Logan. He gave me a chance to really prove myself at TGM." Rich turned to me and put his hand on my shoulders. "I've been there five years now. Damn near kissing six figures. I scored the big accounts and the distributors, and they made me a manager. My accounts generated twice as much revenue as all these young bastards I manage. And I'm working to get TGM the whole enchilada at the new car plant. I'll be rolling in it if I can help pull that one off."

"You're trying to sell me on TGM?" I asked.

"No. You've had your interview. Truth be told, I could

give a damn if you come here or not. I'm just trying to tell you that Logan's one of the good guys and that he helped me out is all."

The dancer Special K had begun to sweat during her performance—the steamy lights and all the pole love had gotten to her. Rich clapped slowly after she finished her routine. She bent over and kissed him, tenderly on the cheek. Her sticky purplish lipstick left a mark on his cheek. She wet her thumb with saliva and cleaned off the smudge. The bouncer glared, but backed off when he saw Rich and Kristen trading smiles.

"Congratulations on your marriage, Rich. I wish it could have been me." From the stripper's mouth, the words seemed like the lyrics to an R&B song. She had a black accented Southern drawl laced with urban attitude, probably the result of some routine exposure to BET. Sweat dripped from her face and onto Rich's. Hunched over, she lost her balance and fell into his lap, draping her arms around him to break her fall. I, a good twelve inches away, smelled liquor on her breath too. The TGM crew laughed it up and copped feels they felt they earned with their generous tips. Special K/Kristen seemed too drunk to care that her body was being groped and rubbed and stroked—violated.

I stepped away from the table as the big black bouncer bursting through the seams of his "Minks Security" T-shirt approached to break up the commotion. The bouncer helped the stripper back up to the stage and ordered the TGM crew to leave, roughing up frail little Stein a bit. Stein smoothed out the wrinkles in his shirt, adjusted his tie, and called the bouncer a "bitch" and the stripper a "stank ho." Rich calmed Stein by grasping his shoulder and massaging them. He gave him an avuncular hug and nodded towards the doorway.

"Ignore him," Rich mouthed to the bouncer. "These young guys, they see some real ass, it goes straight to their heads." The bouncer rolled his eyes and congratulated Rich on his wedding. They shared a soul shake, a bump of the shoulders, and a manly hug.

"This one with you too, Rich?" the bouncer asked, with his eyes fixed on me. I kind of shrugged, crimped my lips, and shook my head in an "it doesn't matter because I was leaving anyway" way. The bouncer reached for my shirtsleeve and guided me to the door. "These fools come here half-drunk every other week," he confided in me. "Feels good to give it to them white boys a little." The bouncer anointed his declaration of superior brawn by flexing an arm muscle, making a tattoo of a silhouetted female body pulsate. I apparently wasn't impressed or amused enough and the bouncer brushed me away.

The TGM crew huddled outside the doorway. Rich appeared disinterested in continuing his bachelor's night out, but Stein and Chuck wrung their hands eagerly, looking to Lou to come up with a plan.

"Time for this boy to really party anyway, so he can forget the hell he's getting himself into," Lou said. "Y'all seen enough droopy fake-ass tits already?"

"You with us, Sam?" Rich asked. "I say we just do the town up right: Eddie Mac's, The Outhouse, The Lollipop Lounge, get blitzed and do some property damage."

The names meant nothing to me; could have been dance clubs, redneck bars, or pickup places—I didn't have a clue.

"No, I don't think so. Early flight tomorrow, you know."

Lou shook my hand. Chuck and Stein headed down the street eagerly, ready for part II of the night's entertainment. Rich lit a cigarette and blew smoke into the breeze, which actually brought a fleeting moment of cool to the stale air. I walked back to the hotel alone, realizing that before graduation rolled around I'd need more options. Affording myself the privilege of choice would require actually having more than one. I began revising my resume in my head, readying myself to send it out a hundred more times the next day.

Lester is Late

(1988)

Waiting for his guests to arrive, A.D. cupped the freshly opened deck of cards, which nested comfortably into the meat of his palm. A new deck held promises of fair hands, camaraderie, and good times. A.D. must have cracked open a hundred of them in over thirty years of playing bridge.

An Army colonel first taught him the basics of the game. In later years, A.D. could barely recall the name of that man, but in thoughts, he often thanked him for the introduction. Bridge required keen insight, teamwork, and real strategy. You'd see little of that in the enlisted men's rapid-fire contests of spades and bid whist, always accompanied by the rote of grunts, gin guzzling, cards slapping on tabletops, and cussing. At the officers' club where he served as an attendant, A.D. spied on the daylong bridge tournaments in which the colonel was a regular participant. There he saw relaxed scotch sipping, smelled the fragrance of long and handsome cigars, and heard lighthearted banter on diverse topics like Eisenhower's golf game or the communist threat in Negro communities. A.D. would watch first, ask questions later, turning each match into a free lesson.

After his stint in the service, A.D. began to fashion

pretend games of bridge with himself, sometimes at home, sometimes in the department store warehouse where he found civilian work. Stealing time between unloading shipments of women's clothing, he showed the game's intricacies to co-worker Lester Waterson. From what they taught each other in the warehouse, A.D. and Lester qualified for and joined the Royales Bridge Club, becoming bridge partners for life.

The club's original bylaws mandated that the Royales meet on the second Monday of every month, unless said Monday was a holiday or a member's birthday. Those were the rules. But as host of the next gathering and with surgery scheduled in one week, A.D. felt recent circumstances had given him license to break the rules, at least once in his life.

The pronouncement of the cherubic female resident physician at the Medical College still echoed in his head: colon cancer. A single lesion spread to the liver. Through a dense fog of confusion, anxiety, and fear, the succession of spoken words after those two all passed like speeding cars on a highway. Prognosis. *Zoom.* Curative. *Zoom.* Outlook. *Zoom.* Survival? *Zoom.*

A.D. seldom caught colds, which he credited to exposure to virulent Asian germs that strengthened his immune system during the Korean War. Life's a trickster, though. This latest health crisis struck without warning, and surgery would be a first for him. Nonetheless, the Royales, he decided, must go on. So A.D. invited the club to his home on a first Sunday, a day of rest reserved for watching television and the life outside the living room picture window.

"Blasphemous!" Lester had blared through the telephone when he got notice of the changed day. "Not

supposed to play no cards on Sundays. But I understand."
Lester's solemnity induced within him a hymnal moan, which
eventually gave way to a reluctant affirmative reply. He was
in, but only if there would be no liquor.

That request was easy to honor. Ever since the seventies,
when the world discovered a correlation between alcohol
consumption and impaired driving, the Royales members
drank less and less hard liquor and even stopped toting
around those meeting mainstays and mini-status symbols:
leather-bound portable bars. No drinking also meant less jive
talk and more focus on the card play, and to A.D. that was
okay too.

"Then it's settled," A.D. had told Lester. "Sunday, my
house, 8 o'clock. Not a drop of liquor will be in the house."
Lester agreed to spread the word to everyone else.

'Everyone' meant six others: two who'd been with the
Royales since its inception, two who'd inherited seats from
past members, and two new recruits, the 'young ones.' It was
A.D.'s own notion that the club should be preserved, to pass
the game on to a restless generation groomed to expect
actual vacations and leisure activities requiring transportation
to distant places or big-ticket equipment purchases.

Only Richard and Dr. McKerrick accepted the aberrant
invite. That was okay. One game of four at one table instead
of two games of eight at two would be better. Less irritation
on A.D.'s ailing colon and a suitable noise level for a Sunday
afternoon. With his guests not due to arrive for over an hour,
A.D. began playing solitaire. It's a sucker's game of chance,
but with the potential for a game-opening breakthrough
resting on the turning over of a single card, it's one that
arouses constant hope. Methodically, A.D. arranged the cards

on the table, pored over his options, and played until the game stalled. He flipped on the TV, landing on an evangelist in the midst of interpreting the story of Job.

"Read the fine print!" the dapper TV minister shouted, waving an open Bible before his mesmerized congregation. "You can't make no contracts with God!" A.D. nodded in agreement as internal body aches pulsed. He turned off the TV. He wrote in a notepad. He watched life outside his picture window. He started another round of solitaire. He flipped cards until the doorbell rang.

Richard showed up first, as he was wont to do. He habitually made much of his effort to disprove the "Negro stereotype." After *his* time in Korea, Richard led a rigid and orderly civilian life—two successful sons, a manageable but not overwhelming number of civic and religious affiliations, and a ranch house with several add-ons coincided with a steady series of promotions at the local social security administration office. Not one for unnecessary conversation, Richard's voice usually shut down soon after congratulating his own time conscientiousness. A.D. offered cheese sandwiches, cut into fours. Richard grabbed a handful and A.D. idled over to the window, desperately waiting for Dr. McKerrick and Lester to arrive.

The row of bungalows in A.D.'s view changed little in the years since he and his Ann first moved to Claiborne Street. Sure, a few tacked on Florida rooms in the aspiring sixties, some daring homeowners experimented with pastels in the optimistic seventies, and the ones who turned rental during the eighties had become a bit rundown. But the picture ostensibly appeared the same as it did when A.D. first hosted a Royales meeting. That time, Ann fixed a spread: turkey casserole, green beans, fresh corn bread, petit fours. Three decades later, with her gone, no children to speak of, and unreliable innards eating themselves away, all A.D. could scrape together were hunks of processed American cheese on slices of Sunbeam bread.

"These are good," Richard said, brandishing mushy sandwich remnants on his fingertips like delicate and prized caviar.

"It's the bread. I just bought it yesterday. Fresh white bread. That's the key." Sarcasm echoed off the picture window, but Richard didn't seem to notice or care. He continued munching, garbling something unintelligible in response.

Just as A.D. glanced at his watch showing the time to be 8:05 p.m., he heard a loud revving from outside, the unmistakable noise of Dr. McKerrick's '74 Cadillac Brougham. The car turned the corner onto Claiborne Street and approached the driveway. A.D. released an exasperated sigh.

"Where's your partner?" Dr. McKerrick said after entering the house and surveying the quiet living room.

"Lester's coming. Have something to eat or drink. There's ginger ale. I bought the Canadian kind you like."

Dr. McKerrick hurried to the buffet, poured himself a drink, then alternately took quick sips and tapped his ring finger on the lip of his glass. He'd inherited his impatience— and his seat in the Royales— from his father. They both had been medical doctors, and whenever someone remarked upon *their* incessant requirements of punctuality, he'd boast that the McKerricks built the most successful medical practice in the area because they respected people's time. It was essentially true, but familiarly, a deflating truer truth lurked in the wings: their success wasn't due to extraordinary customer service or spectacular reputations for skilled doctoring; it was more because the Doctors McKerrick were—for most of their careers—the only black heart specialists in town.

After collecting his sandwiches and glass of ginger ale, Dr. McKerrick headed for the card table, where he deftly began to shuffle the new deck of cards. He recounted his weekend—the activities contained and their order of occurrence probably hadn't changed in years—and he started his own game of solitaire.

The chimes on the old grandfather clock in the corner began to dong, taunting the late start of the game. A.D. pulled a folding chair to the window, sat, lodged his chin into his hands, and looked out for his partner's gold Delta 88.

"Who's doing your surgery?" Dr. McKerrick asked. There was skepticism in his voice. Whoever A.D. told him the surgeon would be, he or she would surely be the wrong one.

"Dr. Myers, at the Medical College."

"Beard? Dark hair? Olive-skinned, Italian-looking fellow?"

"Yeah, that's him."

"You should have gone with the Jew, Cohen. He's better."

A.D. never did like any of Dr. McKerrick's various sides much, not the arrogant fabricator, or the cantankerous complexionist—certainly not the know-it-all. But he did know the local medical community well. Perhaps Cohen was the better choice. Not that they give you much of a choice at the Medical College. A nervous flutter erupted in A.D.'s stomach. He felt light-headed. He gripped his thighs and tried to keep himself balanced in the folding chair.

"You all right there?" Richard asked.

A.D. shuddered. He said nothing.

"Playing cards one week before your surgery. I knew this wasn't a good idea," Dr. McKerrick said. He tightened his lips and shook his head, and, in full doctor mode, helped Richard lift and move A.D. to the recliner. They opened the top button of his collar shirt and, with a dusty, year-old issue of *Ebony* that had been resting on the nearby coffee table, Dr. McKerrick began fanning A.D.

"You'll be all right, just take it easy for a bit," Dr. McKerrick said then ordered Richard, "Get him a glass of ice water. No—make that no ice. Drink that and I'll go look out for that late partner of yours."

"I'm fine," A.D. said. "Stop making a fuss."

Richard brought back a glass of water and a wet paper towel for A.D.'s head. Dr. McKerrick returned to his game of solitaire and Richard made a beeline to the sandwich table.

A.D. feared he'd made his game a disaster. He didn't feel much like playing cards anymore. He wanted Lester to call and say he wouldn't be able to come. He wanted Dr. McKerrick and Richard out of his house. He wanted to be on an operating table getting it all over with. He wanted his Ann.

"What you got here?" A.D. heard Dr. McKerrick say. He then heard the pages of his notepad flipping. A.D. rose up.

"That's personal. You can hand that to me, please."

"Must not be too personal. You got it on the table out there like a signboard out on the highway." Dr. McKerrick continued to flip the pages of the notebook, squinting at A.D.'s shaky penmanship.

"Come on, hand it to me," A.D. said.

Dr. McKerrick held the notepad out with his extended

arm, just short of A.D.'s outstretched hand. The notepad dangled between the two. Dr. McKerrick wouldn't make the extra effort to reach A.D. The pad fell to the floor.

"Could you get that for me, Richard?" A.D. asked.

"What you writing in there?" Richard asked.

"Just hand it to me, will you."

"Makes me no never mind." Richard knelt down, picked up the notepad, and tossed it into A.D.'s lap.

A.D. reclined back into the chair and stuffed the notepad into its cushions. "Let's give Lester a few more minutes. If he's not here, we'll just call it a night."

A sourness sank into A.D. If something were to happen on that operating table, or if the surgery were unsuccessful, his final social experience would be waiting for Lester, in the mustiness of his own house, with the Royales members he liked least. Just before Ann passed, the two of them had taken a cruise. During the trip, she'd remarked on the satisfaction of experiencing nature's most magnificent wonders for the first time and feeling complete for having done so. She saw snow-capped mountains. Touched foreign soil. Witnessed the Midnight Sun and ate exotic foods. Now it was A.D.'s turn, and there he sat with a damp paper towel clinging to his forehead, listening to the hiss of passing cars outside.

"You need to pick a different song," Dr. McKerrick said finally in a resolute tone, suggesting he'd given the diagnosis considerable thought. "More of an anthem to go out on. You'd get the big choir from your church to sing. You don't want no bad soloist messing up on your day. You have to give the people something to feel good about. And our people love the music, of course, so a choir is best."

"What you talking about there, Doc?" Richard asked.

"A.D. here is writing out his funeral. Says he wants a soloist to sing him a spiritual. But I think he should get the choir to sing something more lively. A big rousing anthem." Dr. McKerrick pumped his fist to the downbeats of a rhythm playing out in his head.

"Why you making funeral plans, A.D.?" Richard asked.

"Cause he's scared, that's why," Dr. McKerrick said.

"Just put me in a box and say a few kind things about me right at the gravesite," Richard said. "Afro-American funerals, putting needed insurance money into the ground, folks saying words they don't mean. None of it makes sense to me."

"You got it wrong. Your funeral is the last time the living can show their appreciation for you. It's honorable to do it up," Dr. McKerrick said. "I want the biggest flower arrangements spread all over and the church packed like it was Mother's Day, Easter, and Christmas service all in one."

A.D. listened as Dr. McKerrick and Richard argued their points on appropriate funeral sizes, casket costs, speaker time limits and kinds of prayers to say until Dr. McKerrick asked for a pen and sheet of paper.

"I'll show you a good funeral," Dr. McKerrick said. "The kind I'd want."

"Hand me a sheet too there, A.D. I'll show you mine," Richard said.

Dr. McKerrick and Richard began writing eagerly and earnestly, looking like grandchildren drawing pictures, grandchildren A.D. didn't have and would rather be with. As if racing towards a finish line at the bottom of his page, Richard quickened his pace. Dr. McKerrick put pen to mouth while finishing a thought and then finalized his program.

"There," Dr. McKerrick announced after dotting a final period. "Done."

"Let's see," Richard said.

"No, you first," Dr. McKerrick countered. "It was my idea to begin with."

Richard rose up and began enacting his program. He announced that his eulogy would be read, a Presbyterian minister would preach from whatever scripture he deemed necessary, and then say a prayer for the family, because, after all, that was who the service would really be for anyway. The minister would do ashes to ashes, and everyone would go home for the repast. Short. Dignified. Cost-effective. No unnecessary words spoken whatsoever.

Dr. McKerrick laughed. "The county does better than that at a pauper service. Whether you like it or not, people will want to talk, Richard."

At Dr. McKerrick's funeral, there would be lots of speaking. They'd read citations from friends in high places; a round of two-minute speeches from colleagues and dignitaries would precede the official eulogy and other required religious components, and everyone would march out in song. Dr. McKerrick tried a verse, but his glee got the best of him. Overjoyed and overwhelmed, he toasted his victorious homecoming—and well-lived life—with a glass of Canada Dry.

"Oh, that's just over the top," Richard protested. "You've put undo financial strain on your family for what? To glorify your dead and gone self. Unnecessary. What do you think, A.D.?"

Closer to planning his funeral than either of those two, A.D. pondered which service would be better. He had no family to speak of, so Richard's financial arguments were moot. But how grandiose it would be to celebrate the life of a veteran and a department store warehouse manager—the last title he'd held before retiring—with a service like Dr. McKerrick's. How sad and lonely it would be going out like Richard.

A.D. looked at a framed picture of Ann on the living room wall, hung soon after he took it, and only weeks before her passing. His eyes moistened. He had refused to be bothered with the details of Ann's funeral, leaving that up to her sisters and other relatives of hers. That day, in the stillness of a dark sanctuary sitting on a front pew, a few feet away from the beige and chrome casket, he was an unwilling participant, numbed by selfish questions his then new reality produced: Who would do the cleaning? Could he manage with the loss of Ann's reliable teacher's pension? Who'd cook the meals for the Royales meetings? A.D. could not recall what music they played for Ann. Nor did he remember what words were said.

But he remembered taking that picture of Ann. She posed with hands clasped in front of a vast mountain range stretching across the horizon. Her face aimed downward as if in shy deference to the magnificence around her. The wind blew fiercely, the air chilled their bones. She complained of the cold, and then marveled at it, called it invigorating. "Get as much of the mountains in the picture as you can," she had insisted. A.D. took several shots to ensure the peaks were in view.

The memory preserved was one from life—a good, simple, enjoyed life.

"Well, what's the verdict, A.D.?" Dr. McKerrick asked. He

folded his arms and rocked from side to side. Richard fiddled with his hands in his pant pockets.

Thinking they'd both come up with losing proposals, A.D. closed his eyes, settled his body into the cushions of his recliner, and took a nap.

ACKNOWLEDGEMENTS

Many have provided feedback and editorial guidance on and inspiration for the stories included in this collection. Particular thanks to: My old writing group members Brendan Short, David Taylor and Buzz Mauro who read and reviewed a number of these stories in their earliest stages; the leaders of and participants in writing workshops I attended, including Voices of Our Nation's Arts (VONA) workshops led by Colson Whitehead and ZZ Packer, Hurston/Wright Writers' Week at Howard University, the Sand Hills Writers' Conference at Augusta University, the Jenny McKean Moore Community Workshop at George Washington University and the University of Iowa Summer Writing Festival; the Washington Writers' Publishing House members, especially Melanie Hatter, Kathleen Wheaton and Patricia Schultheis for their thoughtful editorial notes and suggestions; my niece Carolyne M. Banks for her contributions to "Assisted Living"; my niece Sharon E. Williams for her contribution to "Dates with Kreeger"; my sister Dr. Nita Williams Walker for her contribution to "Lester is Late" and my father Tracy E. Williams, Jr. and my mother, the late Willarena Lamar Williams, for filling our home with lots of books and sharing stories about family and growing up in Augusta, Georgia. Thanks also to *The Wrecking Crew*—my siblings Tracy E. Williams, III, Peter W. L. Williams, Serena M. Williams, Dr. Nita Williams Walker, Dr. Mayme Williams Nwaneri and Dollie Williams Banks— who provided general feedback on many of these stories over the years, and to the extended Williams, Lamar and James families—my aunts Claire LaMar Carey and Dr. Carolyne L. Jordan and Careys, Jordans, Robertsons, Joneses, Powells, Parrishes and Russells all—for their lifelong support.

❦

Strivers is set in 11 point New Baskerville type.
The running heads are Copperplate Light and
the titles are Latin MT Std Condensed.

CPSIA information can be obtained at www.ICGtesting.com
Printed in the USA
LVOW08s1619211016

509750LV00004B/661/P